EXE MARKS THE SPOT

SUZY BUSSELL

Snowshoes

Chapter 1

A gust of wind blew around Exeter Cathedral, stirring leaves into a swirl. As it had for the last 600 years, the mighty sandstone building, which had survived the worst Devon weather and Nazi bombs, stood unaffected by the onslaught of the March wind.

Dusk had made the sky pink, with a few high clouds sweeping east. A small group of university students stood talking on the Cathedral Green discussing what to do on their night out. They didn't notice the teenage boy, dressed in jeans and a worn black hoody, who sloped past.

He didn't glance at the cathedral or the students, but trudged on to a narrow walkway that led him onto the high street and its long straight row of shops. A few people milled around outside shops or in the green bus shelters that lined the high street, waiting for a bus to take them out to the rest of the city or beyond to the rural villages.

The teenage boy stopped briefly to peer in a shop window, then moved on. He turned into the alley that led to Northernhay Gardens and walked through the small park hidden behind the rows of shops. He continued through the park until he reached the war memorial.

It took a few moments for a man to appear from the dark cover of an oak tree. He walked towards the boy. 'You're late,' a black baseball cap shaded his face, his hand stuffed into the pockets of his faded tan leather jacket.

'It took longer to walk than I thought.'

'Did you leave your phone at home?'

The teenager nodded.

The man spotted his bag. 'What's in that?'

'Just some clothes and my toothbrush.'

The man nodded. 'Come with me. You've got work to do.'

~

ANGUS DARROW PUSHED his glasses up his straight nose, studied the freshly painted wall in front of him and bent to put the brush down.

His back gave a small protest of pain from all his recent renovation work. In his younger days, he could have carried on all day and evening without feeling tired. But now, having recently passed his fiftieth birthday, it was a different story.

He liked the olive green, though. It would be a smart living room when finished. A small surge of cheerful anticipation ran through him, then dissipated when he glanced around. The rest of the flat was a mess.

In the bathroom alone, the water pipes leaked and the bathroom tiles undulated. The other two flats weren't much better. Several partition walls still needed putting in and carpets had to be laid. At least the electrics were finished. Then he remembered the rest of the flats needed their ceilings and walls painting, not to mention new boilers installing.

It was all going horribly wrong. When planning the renovation, he'd added contingency time for problems, but he hadn't planned for dodgy workmen – or workmen who didn't turn up at all.

There were three flats in all. Previously a pharmacy on the west side of Exeter, it had closed not long after the new oversized supermarket opened nearby. Angus had bought it dirt cheap at an auction, not on a whim but as an investment. He'd been searching for something like it for nearly a year.

He was going to have to do much more of the work himself, that was for sure. He was handy with a set of tools, but the amount of work left was depressing. The project was well over budget, and now he had the additional cost of the mortgage he'd taken out against his own house. He needed the income these flats would provide, and quickly.

His blue, almond-shaped eyes scanned the room and he contemplated what to do next. The list was long. Maybe he should just start doing things instead of thinking about it. That was what he'd learnt in the police, but after twenty-five years, he'd been happy to take early retirement with part of his pension and leave almost a year ago. Being a detective inspector in Plymouth had been beyond stressful. Now all he had to worry about was some DIY.

He tidied up, and was interrupted by a knock at the front door that led into an entrance hall for all three flats from the road outside. Angus walked through and opened it.

'Angus?' It was Tom, an old friend from way back when their daughters were little and in the same class at school. He was dressed in a suit and tie, on his way back from work no doubt. His once-brown hair had a serious amount of grey now. Was it that long since he'd seen him?

He shouldn't be surprised; his own dark-brown hair was turning decidedly grey too. That reminded him: he needed to stop off at the barbers soon. He didn't like his hair too long; it made him look shabby, and he hated shabby.

'Hello, Tom.' The men shook hands. Angus saw specks of tile adhesive and paint on his. He'd need to wash that off.

'How are you?' Angus asked in his usual businesslike tone, as he showed him through to the flat he'd been working on.

'Good, thanks.' Tom looked around, his voice echoing a little in the empty room. 'Coming on OK?'

'Slowly,' Angus replied, unwilling to explain the issues. 'What can I do for you, Tom?'

Tom blinked at him, startled. 'Are you still working as a private detective?'

'I am, yes. I've been taking a bit of a break over the last month to finish these flats, but I've been fielding requests for work. Mainly suspicious spouses wanting their other halves followed, but it brings the money in. Why, are you wanting me to check up on Liz?' Angus smiled as he said it, then realised maybe Tom was here to ask him to do just that.

'No, no, nothing like that; Liz and I are solid. It's about something else. Did you hear about that missing boy, Daniel Cray?'

Angus nodded. 'I did yes.'

'He's my godson.'

'Sorry to hear that.' Angus knew where this was leading. Tom was about to ask him to help find him.

'Yes, well, the police won't do anything. He's eighteen and he left a note, but his parents are sure something's going on.'

'You want me to contact my old colleagues in the police to see if they'll look into it?'

Tom paused a moment before answering. 'Not quite. The police have been round, but there's nothing they can do. Danny left a note saying he was going away.'

'So he's just left home. He can do that if he's eighteen.'

'Yes, but he's autistic. No official diagnosis, but anyone who's met him can spot it a mile off. It's totally out of character. I know him, and he wouldn't do this unless something was very wrong.'

Angus studied Tom's face. He'd known Tom a long time: at least fifteen years. He remembered attending PTA meetings with him, dropping off his daughter Grace at his house for birthday parties and sleepovers. Grace and Tom's daughter Amelie had been inseparable for years. 'You want me to help find him?'

Tom nodded. 'Yeah.'

'I'm not sure I can help. Do his parents know where he might be?'

'They don't have a clue. They're desperate, actually. I wouldn't normally ask—I know you're busy with all this—but they really think something dodgy has gone on. They're willing to pay; they wouldn't expect you to work for free.'

Angus sighed inwardly, but gave nothing away; hiding his emotions was one skill he'd learnt through his job. He really wanted to help, but the work on the flats was pressing, and he couldn't afford to waste time searching for a boy who'd left of his own free will. He wondered how to get out of it—although if they were paying, this could be a way to cover the mortgage and get proper workmen in.

'All right, give me their address and I'll be there tomorrow at 10am.'

Tom patted his shoulder. 'You're a star.'

Chapter 2

The next morning, sitting in his black Volkswagen Golf outside the Crays' house in Heavitree, Angus checked his watch: 9.58am. Their house was near the centre of the city, one of many Victorian terraced houses popular with university students for their location and cheap rent.

He pushed his glasses up his nose, got out of the car, buttoned his suit jacket and rang the bell. He watched for movement behind the frosted glass and tried not to think about the flats and the work still to do.

A woman in her late forties answered the door. No make-up, eyes red and swollen from crying. Her greying hair was pulled back in a ponytail with a few strands falling out.

Angus extended a hand. 'Mrs Cray? I'm Angus Darrow.'

'Thank you so much for agreeing to meet us. Call me Mary.' She took his hand and gave it a limp shake. 'Come in.'

He followed her into the living room at the front of the house. A 50-inch TV dominated the magnolia-coloured room. A large pine coffee table with an aloe vera plant in the middle stood on top of a Persian rug. 'This is my husband, Douglas.' Douglas sat on the settee, a cigarette in one hand, a mug of black coffee in the other. His complexion was sallow and his eyes etched with worry. He nodded but didn't get up.

Angus pulled a small notebook out of his pocket, then sat down in the black leather chair opposite Douglas.

'Would you like tea? Coffee?' Mary asked.

It tempted Angus. He should probably cut down on caffeine, but he'd already given up processed food, most carbs and alcohol. Caffeine was a step too far. 'I've just had a cup,' he lied. He wanted to get down to business. 'So, your son Daniel is missing?'

Mary nodded. 'He's been gone nearly a week, but the police won't do anything.' She pointed to a photo on the wall of a boy, about twelve years old, smiling in school uniform. He was a younger version of the photo being distributed on social media.

'Why's that?'

'He's eighteen and he left a note. They say he's an adult and can make his own decisions.'

'Have you got the note?'

She reached for a piece of paper on the coffee table and handed it to him.

Mum and Dad,

I'm going away, don't try to find me. I'm sorry.

Danny

Short and to the point. 'Is this his handwriting?'

'Yes. Not that he wrote much—he always hated writing and would do anything to get out of it. But that's definitely written by him.'

Angus replaced the note on the table and took a photo

with his phone. 'And do you think he went with anyone else?'

'No. We've asked all his friends, and they are all surprised he's gone away too.' Mary chewed her lip.

'None of them know where he might be? Or that he was thinking of going?'

She shook her head.

'Does he have a girlfriend ... or boyfriend?' Angus wasn't sure how Mary would react to the last part of his question. Exeter was a university city and open-minded, but despite being a cultural hive of diversity, some parts of Devon weren't so forward-thinking.

'If he did, he kept it a secret. He's not gay, I'm sure of it. He's never brought a girl home.'

Angus scribbled notes as she spoke. Just because he'd not brought a girl home didn't mean he wasn't involved with someone. 'And he's autistic?'

Mary nodded. 'They used to call it Aspergers. You're not supposed to call it that anymore. Autistic Spectrum Disorder is the new term. Not that he has an official diagnosis. We tried for years, but the stupid doctors said he wasn't, that there were no obvious signs. They said he was quirky, nothing more, and his head teacher said autism was just an excuse for bad behaviour. They didn't understand him. He's definitely on the autistic spectrum; everyone who meets him agrees. It's obvious.'

Angus had come across enough autistic adults in his police work to spot someone on the spectrum. Most of them hadn't got a diagnosis either but had gone through life always feeling different from the rest of society. As if they didn't fit in. Luckily many were getting help now, mainly through talking to other adults like them.

'In what way is it obvious? It's not that I don't believe

you; it's so that I can try to understand why Daniel would do something like this.'

Mary sat back in the chair and thought for a moment, 'He's obsessive about certain things, to the point of not being able to see or care about anything else. We've always had to tread carefully, otherwise he'd have a meltdown. Not a bad mood like other children: a full-scale meltdown. Total rage. It's like there's a hidden beast inside him that wakes up if we do something wrong.'

Angus nodded as he listened.

'He's always struggled to read facial expressions and social situations. Doesn't get jokes, except slapstick. He's impressionable, much more so than other kids: not street-wise at all. He always did what the other kids wanted. It was so hard at school. He kept getting into trouble for breaking the rules, but it was because the other kids told him to do it.'

Angus sat back, feeling sorry for them. If he'd still been a detective, he'd have got his officers on the case straight away. But he wasn't, and he had to work alone.

He also had to charge them, and looking at their house, they weren't exactly rolling in money. From its slightly shabby appearance, he wondered if they'd be able to pay him. He'd have to ask for some money in advance. But... 'I'm happy to take the case.'

Mary's expression softened and there was a glimmer of a smile. 'Thank you! We have some money saved and we've set up a crowd funder. Send me an invoice and I'll pay it straight away. Tom highly recommended you.'

'I'll need a few days' payment upfront, and I'll give you a progress report every three days. I'd like to see his bedroom and check through his computer.'

Mary got up. 'I'll take you now.'

Chapter 3

Angus followed Mary into Daniel's bedroom and a smell hit him. It was like old cheese, that horrible French stuff his ex-wife Rhona used to love, and which hadn't been in the house since she'd left.

He wrinkled his nose. It was coming up to two years now since they'd gone on a last-ditch attempt-to-save-their-marriage holiday: a week in Malta. At the end, they'd both agreed to part. Telling their daughter Grace had been the hardest thing. They'd sat her down and explained it wasn't anyone's fault but they'd grown apart and it was better they ended it. Rhona moved out and Grace, who was about to start university in York, stayed with Angus until then. He'd bought Rhona's half of the house as part of the divorce agreement.

To say Daniel's room was a mess was an understatement. The dark-blue walls made it dingy, but perhaps it was better he couldn't see it in its full glory, since gaming posters covered the walls. Empty Coke cans were scattered over the floor, the desk and the windowsill. Packets of sweets, plates with half-eaten sandwiches, and clothes littered every surface. He approached the clothes, then backed away. He'd found the source of the cheesy odour.

He remembered being this messy as a teen and driving his parents mad by not cleaning his room, but that was over thirty years ago. These days he was the exact opposite. Ruthlessly tidy in every way, including his appearance. In the police force, Angus had come across many offensive smells and disgusting places – not only people's houses but people themselves. Animals, farms, houses, flats, cars. It was one of the many things he didn't miss.

Mary gave him an apologetic look. 'I know it's a mess, but he won't let me in to clean however much I plead with him. I didn't want to move anything in case there's a clue to where he might be.'

He glanced at her, stifling the desire to tell her clues weren't usually found at the bottom of a Coke can or in an empty packet of crisps. The clothes, however, might hide something. He hadn't brought latex gloves and made a mental note to carry some next time.

'He was so particular when he was little,' said Mary. 'He'd cry if he got dirt on his hands or his clothes. I had to take spares with us everywhere or he'd have a meltdown. That was when I first suspected he was a bit different to other children.'

Angus nodded. He wasn't sure what he was looking for, but he definitely wanted the laptop on the table. 'Do you mind if I take the computer? There might be something on it.'

'Yes, take it. He hardly ever moved away from it; he'd spend every hour of every day on games. He has lots of friends online via some chat thing they all use. Hardly ever met them in real life, though.'

Angus picked up the laptop. 'What about a mobile phone? Or did he take it?'

'He left that, too.' Mary opened a drawer, took it out and gave it to him.

'Bank account?'

'He has a savings account with a building society; the statements are around somewhere.' She spotted a pile of papers on the shelf and handed them to him.

Angus had a quick scan; a few thousand pounds had been withdrawn about a month earlier. 'Do you know why he would have withdrawn his savings?'

'What!' She said in a high pitch then covered her mouth.

He handed her the statement and she stared at it.

'I don't know. I can't believe he's taken all his money. He'd been saving for a new gaming computer. Talked about it endlessly, obsessing over every detail. Bits, bytes, components. I didn't have a clue what he was talking about.'

'Was this all his savings?'

She nodded.

'Had he behaved differently over the last few weeks or months?' Angus powered up the phone. He'd look through it later.

'Not really. We hardly ever saw him after he'd come in from college and eaten his dinner; he just liked to sit in here and play games. He liked strategy fantasy games. There was one in particular he liked, something to do with pirates I think. I can't remember the name.'

'Which college does he attend?'

'He's at City of Exeter College studying a BTEC in Computing. He has a few friends there, but the college said he keeps himself to himself. Doesn't like to be around too many people at once. It's the autism, you see - he likes his own company, or maybe one or two friends.'

Angus nodded and wrote it in his notebook. 'I'll need a

list of his friends and contact details, and the name of his main college tutor.'

Mary nodded. 'I'll do that.'

She left the room and Angus tackled the pile of clothes. Fifteen minutes later, after finding nothing, he walked downstairs and found Mary in the kitchen with another man and woman. 'This is my sister, Janet, and her husband Billy.'

Janet looked older than her sister, but the similarity of their faces was clear in the shape of her eyes and nose. Janet had pixie-cut white hair and immaculate make-up. She wore tight blue jeans and a smart, loose pink shirt. Her husband Billy, however, wore his work uniform: grey trousers and a jacket with 'Exeter Bus Service' embossed on the right side. His belly spilled over the top of his trousers.

'Hello, you're the investigator?' Janet didn't wait for Angus to answer. 'Terrible business. My poor little Danny. It only seems like yesterday I was pushing him around in the pram. He was such a sweet little boy.' She held a packet of cigarettes in her hand and took one out.

'I'll do my best to find him.' Angus assured her. 'Do you know of any reason he would run away?' He watched her light the cigarette with a plastic lighter and take a deep drag.

'None,' she said, puffing out smoke. 'It's all so strange and unlike him. He liked his home comforts.'

'We've been co-ordinating the social media campaign to find him,' Billy said. 'Been a bit of a nightmare trying to get some groups and pages to allow us to post. Apparently some people post pretend missing notices to try and stalk people, so they usually only take posts from the police.'

Angus's eyebrows lifted. 'Has anyone seen him?'

'No. Lots of supportive messages from concerned

people, but nothing to help us find him. They say how awful it must be for us, that they're trying to help, but it doesn't feel that way. Although there was one thing—'

'Go on.'

Billy's eyes shifted to his wife, then back to Angus. 'A couple of parents have contacted me saying their sons have gone missing too. Not at the same time—one was two months ago—but even so. I suppose that isn't too unusual; young people go off on adventures all the time, right? But these were at the same college as Daniel and the same age: just turned eighteen.'

'Did they go together?'

Billy shook his head. 'A few weeks apart, from what I can work out. They didn't know each other, or Daniel, but they left notes too. Apparently they were happy at home and going off was totally out of character.'

'Have the police looked into it?'

'Same thing: the note meant the police weren't interested, and they said the parents needed to let the kids get on with their lives.'

'Can you email me details of the boys and parents please?' Angus handed Billy one of his cards.

'Sure.' He took it put it in his trouser pocket.

'And if there's a sighting, or someone comes to you with anything, however small and unimportant you think it is, phone straight away.'

Janet nodded, then Mary gave a sort of sob and she put her arm around her. 'We'll find him, hon; he'll be back before you know it.'

Angus hoped she was right. 'I've finished in his bedroom for now, so you can tidy it up if you like. Do you know the password for his phone or laptop?'

'He never had a password on the phone, but I don't know about the laptop. Sorry.'

'All right, I'll see what I can do with the laptop if there's a password.' He saw she was clutching a piece of paper. 'Is that the list of his friends?'

She handed it to him. 'His friends from college, his college tutor, and the name of his course. He went to Scouts nearby so I've written details of that, too.'

Angus scanned the list. 'Can you phone his tutor, Mr McInlay, and tell him I want to come in to speak to him and Daniel's friends?'

'I'll do it now,' Mary replied.

'And if you hear from him or any of his friends, call me. I'll keep you updated.'

He knew exactly where to start.

Chapter 4

Back at home, Angus put the kettle on and made himself a cup of tea then sat at the kitchen table contemplating the case. His house was an 80s semi-detached in the Pennsylvania area of Exeter, close to the university and set in a quiet cul-de-sac. He hadn't wanted to move when Rhona left. Some of his family suggested he move up to Scotland to be near them, but he'd lived in Devon since the age of five and he wasn't leaving now. He had friends and ex-colleagues nearby and the thought of moving to Scotland felt like moving to another world.

Angus sipped his tea and wrote in his notebook some reasons a boy like Daniel might leave home suddenly. His parents didn't seem the sort to drive away a child or be the reason behind his departure. Could he be running from abuse? Doubtful, but possible. Or Daniel could have met someone online and gone off with them, maybe. He'd dealt with several cases where young people had fallen in love and done a runner. Lately it was all online, and some were even duped into giving them money. Cat-fishing, they called it, though he wasn't sure why. Or maybe

Daniel had simply wanted to see life outside Devon. London's bright lights drew lots of young people like moths to a candle.

He opened Daniel's laptop. After a few seconds, it sprang to life and a password box appeared. He tried a few obvious ones, but none worked. The screen went blank; the battery had died.

Next he took out the mobile phone. It didn't have a password, but a quick look confirmed that Daniel had wiped it and reset it to factory settings.

He stared at the laptop, taunting him with its blank screen, and closed the lid. He hated computers, and he didn't know how to get past the password. Who was he trying to fool, saying he might be able to get something from the darn thing? The thought of trawling through YouTube videos to try and penetrate its secrets filled him with dread. He didn't have the time or inclination for any of it.

He needed help.

Angus picked up his phone and dialled his ex-colleague DCI Mark Lockwood, or Woody, as everyone called him.

Woody answered straight away. 'Angus, mate, how are you? And how's life outside the force? I bet they're all missing you down in Plymouth.'

'So far so good, thanks. How's things with you in Exeter? Have they made you Chief Superintendent yet?'

Woody laughed. 'You know I'd tell them where to stick their desk jobs, mate!'

Angus stared at the laptop on the table. 'Look, Woody, I need a favour.'

'Course, how can I help?'

'I need to get into a laptop; it's password-protected. A while back, you said you knew someone with tech skills if I ever needed help?'

'Yeah, yeah, you need Charlie. I'll make a call and text you the details.'

Angus smiled. One thing he liked about Woody was that he got to the point. 'Thanks, I appreciate it. It's kind of urgent, though. Can this Charlie do it quickly?' Angus didn't want to annoy Woody, but he didn't want vague promises either.

Woody chuckled. 'No probs at all, mate—Charlie needs something to relieve the boredom. We'll meet up soon, yeah? I'm about to go off on me hols in a week, but in a couple of weeks, yeah?'

'Sure. I'd like that. And thanks again.' Angus put the phone down. While he waited for news of Charlie, he'd go to the college and talk to Daniel's tutor and friends.

ANGUS TRAVELLED into the centre of Exeter. City College was in the middle, close enough for students to walk into the major shopping district. The campus had several buildings, the main one being an ugly 1960s high-rise that dominated the skyline. The place was hard to miss, whatever your opinion of the architecture.

Still, the college was a popular place to study. They offered A Levels and a wide variety of vocational courses. Many students then went and studied at the University a few miles across the city. It was also near one of the railway stations, so many of the students travelled in from other parts of Devon.

Angus found his way through the campus to the computing department, a two-storey building near the main entrance and after asking a student for directions, located Mr McInlay's office.

Angus knocked on the open door, 'Mr McInlay?'

A man of at least sixty looked up from his computer. 'Yes.'

'I'm Angus Darrow. I'm working for Mr and Mrs Cray trying to find their son Daniel. They told you I was coming?'

'Yes, that's right.'

He stood up; he was short, well below Angus's six foot. After a brief glance at Angus behind his glasses, he didn't make further eye contact.

McInlay's office was tiny, and the wall behind the desk taken up entirely by academic books. The window over-looking the courtyard let little light in, so a strip light was switched on despite the sunshine.

'Take a seat,' McInlay said, indicating the chair on the other side of his desk. 'It's a terrible business, to be sure.'

'Do you mind if I ask you a few questions about Daniel?'

'Go ahead.'

'What sort of student is he?'

McInlay pursed his lips and considered for a moment. 'We had no problems with him in terms of unacceptable behaviour. As the main tutor, I'm always made aware of the troublesome ones. I'll check his grades.'

He clicked the mouse a few times, then pressed a few keys on the keyboard. 'His grades are good. Passed every-thing last year and this, and he was on course to complete everything this summer.' He glanced at Angus, 'I do hope he comes back. It would be such a waste after all his work on the course.'

'Daniel's parents believe he has undiagnosed autism. Would you agree?

'They mentioned it to me too, and yes, I agree. I'm no doctor, but I've met enough young people on the spectrum to see definite traits at least.'

Angus got out his notebook and started making a note of McInlay's answers. 'I've been told a couple of other college students ran off in similar circumstances a few months ago. What can you tell me about them?'

'I've not heard of any other students going missing. Who were they?' One of his eyebrows raised in interest.

Angus checked his notes. 'Oliver Smith and Ryan Francis.'

'I'm not familiar with those names. They aren't in my department. Do you know what they were studying?'

'Oliver was studying catering, Ryan, construction. You've not heard the other tutors mention anything?'

'No. But departments don't really mix and college-wide information rarely names students for privacy reasons.'

Angus sat back. 'What about Daniel's friends? His parents gave me a list of the ones they know about, but there might be others.'

'Yes, I'm sure that's the case, most parents don't know what their children get up to here. We have parents' evenings just like schools, but that's mainly for grades and academic issues. You can talk to his class if you like.' He glanced at his watch. 'The next one starts in ten minutes. I'll take you there.'

Shortly afterwards, Angus stood in front of thirty teenagers in a classroom down the hall from McInlay's office. They were mostly boys with a few girls, and a mixed bunch: scruffy and spotty, or in designer gear. Chalk and cheese. They sat in silence as Mr McInlay explained who Angus was and why he was there. None of them appeared to be listening.

'Has anyone heard from Daniel since he went missing?' Angus asked.

There was no reaction at first, then a few kids shook their heads.

'Does anyone know where he is?'

Silence again. One spotty boy in the front shrugged.

'Did Daniel mention to any of you that he was unhappy or thinking of leaving?' Angus wondered if any of them were awake. He could feel his blood pressure rising.

McInlay walked over to stand beside Angus. 'Come on, someone must know something. His parents are really worried about him.'

After more silence, he looked at Angus and shrugged.

Angus faced the class. 'We are all worried about Daniel, since this is so unlike him. If Daniel contacts you or you hear anything about him, or remember something he said that might be relevant, please let me know. I'll leave some of my cards here. Or you can speak to Mr McInlay, and he'll pass on your message.'

Mr McInlay walked to the door, 'Sean and Owen, Mr Darrow wants to speak to you both.'

Two near the back looked at each other, then slowly stood up and walked out into the corridor.

'I'd suggest my office, but it would be rather cramped. Why don't you go to the cafe downstairs and talk there.' McInlay instructed.

The ground-floor cafe was a high-street franchise just like any other, in the middle of the main college building. When Angus had been to college, all they'd had was a coffee machine in the foyer that most people avoided.

Angus bought drinks, then found a table and motioned the boys to sit down. He took a seat opposite, then glanced at the table. Crumbs and a coffee ring. He suppressed the urge to grimace.

He studied the boys, who both had a can of non-diet cola. Sean had thick glasses, a face of acne and greasy brown hair. He wore a faded black T-shirt featuring a heavy metal album cover straight out of the 80s and black jeans. He downed the cola, crumpled the can, put it on the table and sat back, assessing Angus.

Owen sipped from his can. His brown hair crumpled from the snapback cap he'd taken off his head. Angus hated those hats; they made anyone who wore them look dodgy. He was thin, the designer labels he wore draping off his coat hanger-like shoulders.

Angus made a start. 'Daniel's parents told me you were his best friends at college.'

'I wouldn't say that,' Sean said.

'Why's that?'

He shrugged.

'He hung around with us more than anyone else,' Owen said. 'I mean, we sat together in lessons and stuff.'

'Did you hang out when you weren't in lessons?' Angus asked.

'Yeah. Sometimes.'

'You hung around together after lessons, but you weren't friends?'

Sean shrugged again. Owen said nothing.

'So do either of you know where Daniel is?'

They shook their heads.

Angus sighed inwardly. Teenagers were excruciatingly annoying, and these two boys were no different. It was like trying to talk to the dead. 'Did he say anything to either of you about leaving?'

'No,' they said together.

'Do you know any reason why he left?'

They glanced at each other, then both said no.

'What about a girlfriend—did he have one?' Angus asked.

'He asked lots of girls out, but they always said no,'

Sean said. 'He'd have asked a doll out if he thought it would say yes,' Owen sniggered.

'Was there anyone he'd argued with recently? Or got into a fight with?'

Sean answered again. 'Don't think so; he kept his head down. He never had issues with anyone. Too interested in playing computer games.'

Angus rubbed his eyes. This was going nowhere fast; both boys needed more help into adulthood than a college course could provide. He wondered if he'd been this ignorant and apathetic at their age, and made a mental note to apologise to his parents for acting like an idiot when he was a teenager. 'Is there anything you know that might help us find him?'

Silence, then they shook their heads.

'OK. Well, if you hear from him, tell me or his parents straight away. They're really worried. Here's my card.' Angus gave them both his card then stood up. 'Thanks for your time, boys. You can go back to your lesson.'

He left, feeling as though he'd achieved nothing. If those kids knew anything, they weren't about to talk in front of the others. His only hope was for one of them to contact him privately. In the meantime, he would press on with talking to the other people who knew Daniel.

ON HIS WAY back to the car park, his phone rang. It was Daniel's mother.

'Mary, how can I help you?'

'Another child has gone missing,' she blurted.

'Who is it?' He stopped walking, his hand covered his forehead.

'Isabelle Morris. She's in the same Scout troop as Daniel. She's only sixteen so the police are taking it seriously. Her parents phoned me a few minutes ago. They think it's connected. They wanted to know everything about Daniel's disappearance.'

'They think it's connected?'

'I haven't spoken to them about it, but I'm sure it is. How can it not be?'

She had a point. Two teenagers from the same area and the same Scout troop go missing within a week of each other.

'Did she leave a note too?' Angus got into his car.

'Not that I'm aware of. They just said she didn't come home last night.'

That difference stuck in his head. It might be nothing, but it seemed odd.

'Mr Darrow?'

'Sorry, I'm still here. OK. Did Daniel and Isabelle know each other well?'

'I'm not sure. He never mentioned her. He never brought her home or anything.'

'You're certain about that?'

'Yes. He's brought no girl home.'

'Could they have been in a relationship?'

'Not to my knowledge.'

'If you think of anything that might help me find a further link between the two of them, however insignificant, let me know.'

'I will.'

Angus ended the call, then sat in his car and pondered.

He checked the list Mary gave him. With this turn of events, his next visit would be Kenneth Webster, the Scout troop leader.

Chapter 5

Kenneth lived in Pinhoe, on the north-east outskirts of Exeter. The house was a well-manicured detached on a road away from the busy centre. Kenneth clearly wasn't poor. His driveway had plenty of space, but Angus parked on the road.

He walked up the path and rang the doorbell. It made no sound—or at least, the person who rang it couldn't hear if it had rung. So he knocked too.

The door opened, and an elderly man peered out. He was wearing brown trousers and a jumper with a shirt underneath.

'Kenneth Webster?'

'Yes.'

'I'm Angus Darrow, and I'm looking into the disappearance of Daniel Cray. His parents have hired me to find him. Do you mind if I ask you some questions? You are Daniel's Scout leader, aren't you?'

'I am, yes. Come in.'

Angus followed him through to the living room and felt

as if he'd stepped back thirty years. Magnolia walls and flowery curtains with a matching rug. Laura Ashley had done well from Kenneth back in 1985. Kenneth walked over to a TV in a mahogany cabinet, switched it off and closed the doors. 'Do sit down.'

Angus sat on the sofa, and Kenneth went to his electric-powered recliner. On the other side of the room was a desk with a large computer screen displaying a local car mechanic's website.

Angus indicated to it, 'Having car trouble?'

Kenneth looked over to it, 'No - just the MOT.' He smiled curtly.

'It's a grim business.' Kenneth shook his head. 'Daniel never seemed the sort of boy who would run away.'

'How well do you know him?'

'He's been coming to Scouts for a long time: years. Now let me think, at least four or five years.'

'Does he mix well with the others?'

Kenneth pondered for a moment. 'Daniel's different from other boys. He prefers his own company and he's shy, but he seems to enjoy it. He's not the type of boy who'd come along if he didn't like it.'

On the dresser was a large photo of scouts lined up at what looked like a camp. He was too far away to see if Daniel was in the photo. The other photos seemed to be of family members, most likely his children and grand-children.

'Was Daniel close to any boys or girls?'

'Not really. Nothing that sticks out.'

'Anyone he didn't get along with?'

'No.'

Angus took out his notebook. 'I take it you've heard Isabelle Morris has gone missing?'

There was no pause. 'Yes, that's terrible. Two of them now. Mrs Cray just phoned to tell me.'

'How well did they know each other at Scouts? Did they talk much?'

'You think their disappearances are connected?'

'I don't know; that's why I'm asking you.' Angus fought to control his tone.

Kenneth considered. 'I don't think there was a friendship. The girls all stick together, which I suppose isn't unusual.' He sighed. 'I don't like girls there. It changed the entire atmosphere of the group when they allowed them to join. Sometimes boys need spaces away from girls.'

Angus thought for a moment about whether he agreed. He had a daughter, and he'd have been pretty annoyed if a scout group had banned her just because she was female. He didn't say anything though. Personal opinions were best kept to yourself when interviewing someone. 'So you didn't see any sign that the two of them were in a relationship?' The clock on the mantlepiece chimed, interrupting Angus's thoughts. 'How long have you been a scout leader?'

'Over forty years now.' Kenneth puffed up his chest. 'It's been an enormous part of my life. I was in that troop when I was a boy, and I've been leading it for decades now. But it's changed a lot since I started. We used to be able to get lots of volunteer helpers from the community, but these days we have to get background checks. That takes weeks and most people can't be bothered.' He paused for a moment. 'I don't think there shouldn't be safeguards, but it's got to the point where it's putting people off.'

'You've seen a lot of boys come and go then, over the years.'

'I have. Some have gone on to great things. Some, not so much.' He shrugged.

'What do you think of Daniel? Is he destined for greatness?'

'He's a nice enough boy. Causes no trouble. Bit obsessive about things, but that's not unusual.' He thought for a moment. 'It's difficult to tell how he'll be when he's grown up, though at eighteen I suppose he technically is. But he's very young for his age, in maturity I mean.'

'His parents believe he's on the autistic spectrum. Would you agree?'

Kenneth smiled. 'I'm not a doctor, so I couldn't say. We're all on the spectrum, though, aren't we? Some more than others.'

Angus looked at his notepad; he'd got through most of his questions. 'As you've been a Scout leader all that time, you must have come across a lot of kids on the autistic spectrum.'

'A few.'

'And?'

'Well, he certainly had characteristics of it. He was awkward in social situations.'

'Did he get bullied?'

'I never saw any, and we don't tolerate bullying in the troop. We have a strict code; I can show you if you like.' Kenneth made to stand up.

'It's all right, I don't need to see it.' Kenneth sat back down. 'Daniel's parents mentioned he never went to scout camps. Is that unusual?'

'That's right. Daniel didn't want to sleep away from home, so he never went on any of the camps or anything else that involved staying the night. That's why it's so strange that he's run away. He wouldn't even go to camp for the badges. You see, you can only get some badges when you're away on camp, and Daniel enjoyed collecting them. He wanted as many as possible; it was a sort of obsession. I think that's why he kept coming so long—he wanted all the badges. His mother always said he'd go one day, but he always refused.'

Angus leaned forward. 'Did Daniel tell you he was running away?'

'No.'

'Did he mention any reason to you which might explain it?'

'No.'

'Can you think of any reason Daniel might have run away, then?'

Kenneth shifted in his seat. 'I'm sorry, but no. I can't help. I just can't understand it. He didn't seem to be the sort of boy to do that. He's very close to his parents.'

They sat in silence for a few moments. Kenneth seemed to be waiting for Angus's next question, and Angus couldn't think of anything else he needed to ask. 'OK,' he said, at last. 'If you think of anything that might help to track him down, or if he contacts you, please call me straight away.' Angus took out a card and handed it over.

'I will, and I hope you find him.'

Back in his car, Angus reviewed everything so far. When he'd been in the police, he'd always worked method-ically with every investigation. It had served him well and this was no different. He took out his notebook and re-read the notes he'd taken a few minutes earlier, then thought about Kenneth's reactions and demeanour during the interview. There wasn't anything that indicated he was lying. He seemed to be as concerned as everyone else that Daniel had gone missing. He'd start again in the morning with his next line of enquiry.

When Angus got home, Daniel's laptop and phone

were still on the kitchen table, taunting him. He remembered he hadn't had a reply from Woody about Charlie. If
Woody hadn't replied by the morning, he'd send him a text
to try to hurry him along.

Chapter 6

Angus did text Woody in the morning, and ten minutes later, Woody replied:

Sorry for the delay—Charlie goes off grid sometimes. You can go now. Address is Fortescue House, East Street, Topsham.

Topsham, thought Angus. He knew it: a small town a short drive south of Exeter along the Exe estuary.

It was where all the rich people lived.

His sat nav directed him to the address. He drove onto the gravel driveway and parked next to what was presumably Charlie's car: a dark-blue Bentley.

Fortescue House sat in an elevated position overlooking the River Exe. A posh name, a posh house. A stone plaque built into the brickwork dated it as 1879.

Angus rang the doorbell and waited. Nothing.

He pushed his glasses up and rang the bell again, leaning on it for a few seconds this time. He pulled his phone out of his coat pocket and sent another text to Woody.

You sure Charlie is home? There's no answer. He typed.

Just keep ringing the bell. Charlie is at home. Came the reply a moment later.

Charlie wasn't answering. He needed the laptop analysed as soon as possible, and he didn't have a contingency plan. He didn't relish going to the techie boys he'd worked with in the police; they'd probably laugh at him. All the officers called them anoraks; not to their face, but of course they'd know. He was about to try hammering at the door when he heard two locks clicking and the snick of a bolt. At long last, the door opened.

A woman peered blearily back at him. She was in her mid-forties, with blonde shoulder-length hair all over the place and yesterday's mascara around her brown eyes. She wore pyjama shorts and a white T-shirt which said 'Beeee Happy'. Angus tried not to stare at her slender legs, or her hips. He would have looked her in the eye except that her hair almost hid them.

'I've come to see Charlie. Woody sent me,' Angus explained.

'Come in,' she croaked in a southern English accent.

He followed her through the high-ceilinged hallway to the lounge, carefully stepping over discarded clothes, beer cans and wine bottles as he went.

She plonked herself down on a deep-red Chesterfield sofa, crossed her legs and stared at him through her hair. 'What do you want?'

'I told you. I'm here to see Charlie. It's about a laptop.' He tried not to sound snappy; it wasn't her fault he was having a bad day. Though she certainly wasn't helping.

'I'm Charlie,' she stated.

He stared at her for a moment. 'Ok...' He thought about the brief conversation with Woody yesterday. At no point had Woody said that Charlie was a man. He'd just assumed. 'Short for Charlotte?'

'Yep. Sit down.' She indicated the seat behind him, which matched the sofa. He obeyed, moving the empty pizza box first.

She pulled her blonde hair into a rough ponytail, revealing her brown eyes and fine-featured face. 'Woody only calls me Charlie because he knows it annoys me. Everyone else calls me Charlotte. Or they do if they want to stay friends with me and get me to do things for them.' She blinked twice. Slowly and deliberately. Her voice was deadpan, but her eyes glinted and the corner of her mouth curved into a smile.

She held all the cards and they both knew it. Dealing with difficult people was part of the job in the Police, so if she was going to be like that, he was ready.

Angus cleared his throat. 'Well, Charlotte, I've got a laptop and a phone and I need you to get everything off them. The owner is a young man who's missing and his parents are worried.'

He unzipped the computer bag he'd brought with him, took out the laptop and phone and passed them to her.

'Isn't it a police matter? Missing person?' She opened the laptop and waited for it to spring to life. Nothing happened.

'He left a note saying he was leaving, but he's vulnerable.'

She lifted the computer and examined the outside. 'The battery's dead.'

'Is that a problem for you? Look, Woody said you could help me get everything off it.'

She sighed. 'Yeah, he said someone would be round. Fucking Woody. Wait here.' She stood up and padded out of the room.

Angus watched her leave then looked around the room. He searched for a word to describe it and came up with opulent. It looked like something out of a style magazine, except for the pizza boxes and wine bottles. Was she the owner or was she house sitting and trashing the place at the same time?

Charlotte returned a few minutes later with a charger and two Alka-Seltzer fizzing in a glass. This time she went to the desk in the corner. She plugged in the laptop, then downed the drink.

A few moments later, the laptop sprang into life, the startup tune chiming loudly. 'Ouch.' She turned down the volume.

'What's going on?' said a deep voice from the doorway. It belonged to a man in his mid-thirties wearing nothing but a pair of blue boxer shorts. He ran a hand through his tousled hair. 'I thought you were coming back to bed.' He motioned his head suggestively, then frowned when he saw Angus. 'Who's he?'

Charlotte didn't look up. 'He is none of your business.'

'So you're not coming back to bed?'

'Sadly, no. I've got to work. You'll have to leave.' Her voice was curt, businesslike.

'That's a shame. I was hoping we could do that thing again. You know, like last night…' He raised his eyebrows.

Charlotte gave a dismissive wave of her hand. 'Sorry, but no. Got important things to do with this laptop.'

The man didn't move. 'Any chance of coffee and breakfast?'

That made her look up. She sighed and stared at him for a few seconds. It reminded Angus of how his daughter Grace had looked at him when she was in her early teens and didn't want to help with the washing up. He suddenly missed those days.

'There's a cafe down the road which serves all that pretentious breakfast stuff. You know: bagels, smashed avocado on toast, granola. Things like that. I highly recommend it.'

The man sniffed. 'All right then.' He wandered off.

Charlotte glanced at Angus. 'Have you checked the computer?'

'I couldn't get past the login screen even if I wanted to. I'm no good with technology.'

'Easy when you know how.' She smiled. Her voice had softened.

He was briefly reminded of the techies in the police. They'd all had a similar 'I'm cleverer than you' attitude towards him and his officers. But they'd mostly been blokes, and somehow that comment, coming from an attractive woman lost its sting.

He didn't care what she was doing to the laptop to get into it, he was just grateful he wasn't trying to do it himself. He'd been around long enough to see the evolution of the internet. As it has become more popular, it had spawned different crimes. Crimes online: hate crimes, data theft, fraud, a new type of voyeurism, phishing, viruses. Viruses were colds or flu, not malicious software, for goodness' sake.

He avoided social media as much as possible. He'd tried Twitter briefly, then quit when he realised it was a cesspit and he wasn't missing out on anything except drama, arguments, hate and photos of people's dinners. Oh god, the photos of people's dinners. Why did anyone do that?

His daughter Grace had tried to get him to join Instagram. 'It's a great way to stay in touch, Dad.' But he always declined her offer, not even allowing her to download the app onto his phone. He was happy enough to look through her photos when they met up.

A few minutes later, the man reappeared in the doorway, this time wearing jeans and a shirt. 'Well, er, thanks for last night. It was ace. We should do it again soon, yeah?'

'Bye,' she answered with a fake smile.

He turned to go, then stopped. 'Have you got my number?'

'No.' She carried on typing.

He fumbled in his jacket pockets, then held a card out to her, but she just looked at it. After a few moments, he put it on the desk next to her. 'Call me, yeah?'

She didn't respond.

'Bye, then.'

As soon as the front door had closed behind him, Charlotte picked up the card, tore it in half, and dropped it into the small wicker bin beside her.

Chapter 7

Charlotte glanced at the man she'd let in a few minutes before. She hadn't even asked his name. Had Woody mentioned it when he called? She couldn't remember. The phone call had been brief and hazy, as he'd woken her up. Even worse, he'd told this man her name was Charlie. He knew she hated being called Charlie more than anything else in the world. Well, except maybe her ex-husband, Idris. Oh, and Michelle, her former best friend whom Idris had cheated on her with. She hated them both equally.

Her head pounded and she felt shaky; she really had to stop drinking so much. The hangovers were much worse now that she was over forty.

The man was smart in a dark blue suit, a white-and-blue checked shirt and a dark burgundy tie. His hair was greying, but short and well-cut and he'd shaved that morning. His glasses looked like a designer brand. In fact, he was rather handsome.

She dragged her attention back to the laptop. The user login screen came up, and she tried a few obvious passwords: 'Letmein', 'Password', '123456'. None worked. She switched on her computer and linked it to the laptop; her password cracker would break it easily.

In less than a minute, it had found it.

'I'm in.' She turned and smiled at the man. 'His password is FireBoy123. Capital F, capital B.'

She watched as he wrote it in his notebook. 'Longer passwords are usually harder to crack, but the numbers and no special characters meant the length of the password didn't really matter. This one was easy.'

He pushed up his glasses and smiled.

'What's your name?' she asked.

'Angus Darrow.'

'So what are you after, Angus Darrow?'

He came over and stood next to her. 'I need emails, online chat, internet history. Everything that might help me to find him, or explain why he left.'

'You said he left a note for his parents. Do you have it?'

Angus took out his phone and showed her the photo he'd taken of it the day before.

'His handwriting is atrocious. Kids these days can't write properly.' She pondered. 'It doesn't give any details, does it? It'll take a while to go through this. Are you OK to wait?'

He nodded and sat back down. A moment later, the front door opened and closed.

'That will be Helena.' Charlotte said, not looking up. She plugged a removable disk into the laptop and copied the contents of the hard disk onto it. Her disk analysis tools would find everything he was looking for.

High heels clicked on the hall floor until Helena appeared in the doorway. She was wearing leggings, and a cropped top which showed off her slim figure, and was perfectly made up. She scanned the room, then frowned.

'Who he?' She pointed at Angus. Her thick Eastern European accent was even more pronounced than usual. 'You sleep with random man again?'

'Morning, Helena,' Charlotte smiled at her. Helena looked around the room, frowning. She wouldn't be happy when she found out about Gary or Craig or whatever his name was. She'd met him in the pub last night, and somehow they'd ended up back here.

Helena came into the room and began picking up the litter. 'How many times I tell you no sleep with random man?' She turned to Angus. 'You go home.'

Angus stared at her.

'Relax, Helena. I haven't slept with *him*, he's here for work. Nothing more.'

Helena's expression relaxed, then her eyes narrowed. 'You did had man here though. How many times I tell you?'

Charlotte stopped typing and turned around. 'We'll discuss it later.' Much later, hopefully.

Helena harrumphed, then went to a speaker and switched it on. Classical music drifted into the room.

'You vant drink?' Helena asked him.

'Er, coffee would be great, thanks.' He smiled.

Helena nodded, then left the room.

'Sorry about her,' said Charlotte. 'She's a close friend and my housekeeper too, and she's just looking out for me. Her bark is worse than her bite.'

A few minutes later, Helena returned carrying a tray loaded with enough coffee and croissants for two.

'You're an angel,' Charlotte said, and kissed her on the cheek. Helena smiled, then left the room picking up litter as she left.

Half an hour later, she turned to Angus. 'It's a classic case of sextortion, I'm afraid. He gets friendly with a girl online, they talk for a few weeks, then she persuades him to do a sex act on camera, yada yada yada. She recorded it, then blackmailed him. From what I can gather, it's recent.'

Angus nodded.

'She sent him messages on a live chat forum two weeks ago; that's when it started. When he stopped answering her demands and blocked her, she emailed him. She sent him a copy of what she'd recorded–not all of it, but enough to convince him they had something on him. I'm assuming she's a she, but no doubt there's a gang behind it. There always is. The video isn't on here, but I'm guessing that whatever he did, he won't want it out there.'

She paused for a moment. 'Actually, there are plenty of videos like that on the internet, but obviously he'd know it was there, and it would be there forever.' She shook her head as though to stop herself from rambling.

'Is there any sign of where he might have gone?' Angus asked.

'I haven't found anything yet. I'm still checking through the chats on Discord.'

Angus looked blank.

'All the kids use it to communicate; it's a chat forum. They can speak to each other as well as send text, and there was plenty. He deleted lots of emails on his computer, but I hacked into his account on the server and found the originals. Luckily, he'd been using IMAP protocol for his email, so they only deleted on his laptop and not on the mail server. Schoolboy error.' She gave a small shake of her head.

Angus sat back in the chair. 'I have no idea what you are talking about.'

Charlotte smiled at him. 'Use technology but don't care how it works, huh?'

'Pretty much.' He pushed his glasses up his nose.

She continued, 'Anyway, there's not much in them. I found several messages showing that they'd met in person before this, so the gang bent over backwards to get him to trust her.' She frowned. 'The strange thing is that normally, with this type of sextortion, they get some money from the victim and that's it. But they wanted him to do something else as well as give them money.'

'He withdrew all his savings a couple of weeks ago. In cash.'

'What date?'

Angus took out his phone and found the photo he'd taken of Daniel's building society statement, 'Tuesday 4th November.'

'That fits the timeframe. I'll keep checking and see what else I can find.'

'The emails might hold a clue.'

'Not for the missing money. None of the emails from the girl tell him to give them money. They tell him to delete his emails, wipe his phone, leave home and go to Northernhay Gardens in Exeter. I'll put everything you need to see on a USB flash drive so you can look at it to your heart's content.'

'Thanks.'

She left the room and came back a couple of minutes later with a flash drive and handed it to him. 'Do you know Northenhay Gardens?'

'Yes, I live in Exeter – have done for the last twenty years. It's the gardens directly behind the main shopping area. A hidden treasure.'

'I'm not sure about CCTV, but it is closed at night. There are two entrances. CCTV should make it easy to see who he met then.'

He nodded. 'That's excellent work. Thank you.'

'Of course it is. That's why Woody sent you to me.' Charlotte smiled at him. 'So, how long have you been out of the police?'

He stared at her. 'Woody told you?'

'No, but you have police written all over you, although you dress smarter than most and if you were still in the force you'd have minions to do this kind of thing for you.'

'I left just over a year ago.'

She was right then. 'Woody is so stressed. I'm always telling him to quit. He could come and work for me, but he thinks he's saving the world. Well, a small piece of Devon, anyway.'

'I miss the camaraderie of the police, but not the stress.'

She inspected him. Yes, he was rather handsome. And if he was a friend of Woody's, he was a decent bloke. Woody didn't associate with anyone even slightly dodgy these days. 'Is that what made you leave? Stress?'

'I'd had enough after twenty-five years. I'm glad to be out of it.'

'But still investigating. Did you work with Woody?'

He nodded. 'I was in Plymouth, he's Exeter but our paths crossed regularly. Meetings and working together sometimes. How do you know him?'

Charlotte tilted her head a little. 'Can't you tell?' She blinked at him a few times. 'Charlotte Lockwood.' She held out her hand to him and he took it briefly.

'You're related to Woody?'

'Yep, I'm his little sister.'

'Really?' He scanned her face.

'You're surprised. We definitely have the same parents. And I definitely remember growing up with him and being the annoying little sister. All that sort of stuff.'

'He must be a fair bit older than you.' He sat forward and smiled.

'Seven years.'

He nodded. 'That's quite an age gap.'

'Making him an old git, and me not so old,' she said brightly. 'Anyway, now we're all grown up, the age gap is nothing.'

'He never mentioned he had a sister.'

'Really? I must have a word with him about that.' Her lips twitched.

'He doesn't talk about his family, apart from Fiona.'

Charlotte smiled. 'She's the sister I always wanted, and they're perfect together. They always have been.'

Fiona had been more than a sister-in-law, especially when Charlotte's marriage had collapsed in a steaming pile of pain and hurt. She didn't think she could ever repay Fiona for being a combination of sister, mother and best friend at her greatest time of need. Charlotte shook herself; she needed to stop thinking about her ex-husband. 'Well, whatever has happened to this boy, it doesn't look good.'

'I think he's in danger,' said Angus. 'I need to find him, and quickly. His parents believe he's on the autistic spectrum, and his college tutor agrees.' He paused. 'If I give you my card, will you tear it up and put it in the bin too?'

She laughed. 'No, but why would I want to call you?'

'I'll need your help again. I'll need your number.'

'Oh no, my debt to Woody is repaid.'

'He told me you might say that. But he says you owe him more than a laptop analysis.'

'Bastard. Woody, not you. OK, I'll give you my number. And I'll take your card, and promise not to rip it up. All because of my dear brother.'

Angus offered his phone, and she typed in her number

and gave it back. He dialled the number and her phone rang. 'Just checking.'

'I could just block you.' There was a note of sarcasm in her voice.

'But you won't.'

Chapter 8

Charlotte watched him leave the room and suddenly realised she should see him out. She followed and watched as he got into his car, then shut the door and dialled her brother's number. 'Tell me everything you know about Angus,' she demanded the moment he answered.

'Hello to you too, little sister,' said Woody. 'You liked him, then?'

'He's rather lovely,' she replied in a dreamy voice. Then it changed to concerned. 'He must think I'm a total slob though. When I answered the door, I had bed hair and I was in my PJs. Not to mention the bloke from last night who was here, pizza boxes, wine bottles…'

He laughed. 'I thought you'd take to him. He's a good man: the best. That's all you need to know for now. Be nice to him.'

'When am I ever not nice?'

'You helped him, I take it?'

'I did. But you made me.'

'You would have done it anyway. But your debt to me isn't repaid; you still owe me.'

She sighed, remembering the huge favour he'd done her. Her ex-husband Idris and her ex-friend Michelle had been setting out for their honeymoon when Woody pulled some strings at Passport Control in Italy. Inexplicably, a contact of Woody's had questioned Idris and Michelle for twelve hours, including carrying out body cavity searches.

'So he said. You're such a stickler. I don't mind seeing him again, though. He has amazing blue eyes. Is he married?'

'Not anymore.'

'Girlfriend?'

'Not that I'm aware of.'

'That's made my day.'

Woody chuckled again. 'What was it all about, then?' he asked.

Charlotte explained what Angus was investigating and what she had found.

'It will give you something to do, won't it? You've been wallowing too long; you need a distraction.'

'That's what my therapist keeps saying—have you been colluding with her? Look, are you coming over for dinner someday soon?' she asked.

'I'll check with Fiona. But you know you can come over whenever you like, too.'

'I know.'

She heard someone in the background wherever Woody was. 'Sorry, got to go. I'll talk to you soon.'

Charlotte put the phone down, stood up, and stretched. She definitely needed a bath. Last night had been enjoyable with whatever-his-name-was, but it was just sex. He hadn't seemed so attractive in the morning, when she was sober. Anyway, she didn't want a relationship yet. She was still reeling from Idris.

She'd been with him since the last year of university,

then they got married and had two amazing sons. Oh, and set up a cyber-security business. Fifteen years later, having sold the business for £200 million, they'd planned to sail off into the sunset together and explore the world. But he'd sailed off into the sunset with someone else: her former best friend Michelle. Bastard. At least she had half the money. She'd moved to Devon to be near her brother and his wife, leaving London and her wounded heart behind. She'd bought the house in Topsham after making the owners an offer they couldn't refuse. The house had been her great-grandmother's years before and she had fond memories of visiting every summer when she was growing up. When she'd passed away, it had been sold. Well, it was hers now, and the only way she'd ever leave it was in a wooden box.

Charlotte sat on the side of the bath, watching the water flow into the tub, then added Epsom Salts.

The missing boy's parents must be distraught. She'd have gone mad if her own boys Gethin and Rhys had gone missing. Luckily they were both grown-up now, and with parents who were cyber-security experts and an uncle who was a police officer, they'd been well aware of any dangers.

She'd enjoyed going through the laptop; it had made her feel useful again, given her a purpose. The terms of the sale of the cyber-security business included a competition clause that meant she couldn't work in the same field for five years, and there were still three and a half years left to go. But voluntary work was something else. She could definitely do investigative work for a private detective as long as he didn't pay her.

She'd liked Angus; he wasn't classically handsome but good-looking men were often arrogant. There was something calming about his presence. And those blue eyes…

Helena entered the bathroom. 'I finished cleaning up

mess from last night. You have man here again…' She stared at her, her hand on her hip.

'I know, I know…'

'You be careful or you catch zomething.' Helena wagged a finger at her.

'We were careful—'

'Good. But you need nice man to marry and stop acting like slut.'

If anyone else had said that to Charlotte, she'd have been offended. But Helena was her most beloved wing-man–or rather, wing-woman. Charlotte had been there for Helena, too, when she had been living with a violent part-ner. She knew Helena only wanted the best for her, she trusted her completely, and she liked her being around.

'Anyway, I'm not a slut,' Charlotte replied, 'I'm just extra horny because of perimenopause and there's a never-ending supply of men willing to oblige. And Ross is out of the country at the moment.'

Ross was her friend with benefits. At 35, he was 10 years younger, but he didn't seem to mind sex with an older, more experienced woman. Their relationship came without strings attached. No commitment, no going out in public together, just sex whenever she wanted it. That was always how it worked–whenever she wanted it. Ross had never turned her down yet.

'Vell, you must stop zis. It no good. Find nice man to marry and have sex when you vant. I have friends in Romania who help you find husband.'

'I don't need help to find a husband. I don't want to get married again.'

'He be nice man. We no tell him you have millions of money and he love you for being you.'

'You're so sweet, but no.'

'It not right, woman on her own.'

'You're single,' Charlotte pointed out.

'I don't count. Too old for man now,' Helena said, with an expressive wave of her hand.

'You're only a few years older than me!'

Helena made a sort of snort. 'I know.' She shrugged and left.

A moment later, Charlotte's phone rang. The display told her it was Angus from earlier.

Chapter 9

When Angus left Charlotte's, he pondered whether to try the pretentious cafe she'd mentioned to that man, but headed home for food instead. It would be much easier to make something that fitted in with his new fitness regime than wade through the sort of unhealthy menu cafe's served, and he knew his willpower faded the hungrier he got. If he went home, he could check on the flats and see if the workmen had made progress, or even turned up.

Back in his house, he loosened his tie, then took off his jacket and hung it up, smoothing down the creases. As he put the kettle on, his phone rang. The display said *Rhona*.

'Angus, I need to speak to you about Grace's twenty-first,' she said the moment he answered.

'Hello, Rhona. I'm fine, how are you?' he said in a patronising tone.

'Look, I'm organising a twenty-first birthday party for Grace and you're invited. I know it's late notice, but she's only just told me she was coming back to Devon for it.'

That had made his day. He'd thought he'd not get to see Grace on her birthday. 'Where is the party?'

'At the new community hall in Pinhoe. Nothing fancy, but there'll be food and a disco. It was all I could get at such late notice.'

Angus knew the place. The local community had raised the money for it over several years; the previous building had been a dilapidated Scout hut.

'I need you to contribute,' Rhona continued.

'How much?' His voice had a note of suspicion.

'Not sure yet. A few hundred, but I'll let you know.'

'All right.' Angus frowned. He loved his daughter very much, and he'd give her his last bit of money if she needed it. But Rhona's 'nothing fancy' would inevitably turn into something very fancy and also expensive.

'Thanks, Angus. I'll speak to you soon. I've got to go, council meeting in a minute. Bye.' She put the phone down before he had a chance to say goodbye back.

Rhona had been a Devon county councillor for ten years now. He'd been proud of her when she was first elected, but the long hours—hers and his—had taken its toll on their marriage.

Angus stared ahead. He had known Grace's twenty-first was coming up, of course, but he'd hoped they'd celebrate with a simple family dinner during her break from uni. Just being with his daughter was enough. He'd also have to think of a present: something she could keep. She'd probably appreciate money being at university, but he was always slipping her bits here and there, just in case. He knew it was a bad habit. His father told him he should let Grace stand on her own two feet. But if he had the world, he would give it to her.

Angus's phone rang again, and this time it was a mobile number he didn't recognise. 'Hello?'

'Mr Darrow? This is Sean—we met at college yesterday. It's about Daniel. I remembered something…'

It was what Angus had hoped for: one of Daniel's friends contacting him. 'Go on.' He tried to sound encouraging; teenagers could get so touchy.

'It might not be relevant, but I'm the only one he told.'

'Tell me anyway.'

'Daniel was having extra tuition for his college work. He had an IT tutor.'

'A private tutor?'

'Yeah, they met every Wednesday afternoon in a cafe. I'm not sure which one.'

Angus got out his notebook. 'You said that nobody else knew. I assume you mean just his friends?'

'No, not even his parents. He was struggling with the course and he didn't want them to know.'

'Why didn't he tell them?'

'He didn't want them to worry. He was falling behind with work and just needed a bit of extra help. He said he didn't want them knowing because they worried too much already.'

'Do you know how he was paying for the tuition?'

'No. He doesn't have a Saturday job or anything. Maybe he paid him with pocket money or savings.'

'Do you know the tutor's name?'

'David something. I'm not sure of his surname, but Daniel said he was local. I think he found him on a tutor website.'

'OK, thanks. If there's anything else you think I should know, call me.'

Angus ended the call, made a note of the tutor's name, and immediately rang Charlotte.

She picked up the phone after one ring. 'Hello, Angus,' she said brightly. 'Checking I've not blocked you again?'

'Not at all. One of Daniel's friends just called and told me that Daniel had a private tutor. I know you went over it, but can you remember anything on his computer that mentioned one? He needed help with his computing course at college. First name's David.'

'Not that I can remember. I'll double check for you. David, you say?'

'Yes.'

A pause. 'OK, I'll check and phone you back either way.'

'Thanks.'

Chapter 10

Charlotte put the phone down. She hadn't been expecting to hear from Angus again so quickly. She'd copied the contents of Daniel's laptop onto an external hard drive earlier so that she'd be able to analyse the data much more quickly. Then she'd written several computer programs to analyse the data, so much of the work was just leaving the program to it. She'd developed the analysis toolkit years ago; it needed tweaking occasionally, but it still worked a treat. She'd do it after her bath.

An hour later, she'd completed the task and was ready to call Angus, but first she went to the kitchen to find Helena.

'That man from this morning phoned again,' she stood next to Helena.

'Mr Angus?' Helena looked up. She was stirring something in a bowl.

'Yep. He needs my help.'

'Not good, not good. England supposed to be safe place for kids.'

'We've always had crime, Helena.'

She shrugged. 'Pah. I know, but less than some places.'

'Is that cozonac you're making?' Cozonac was Charlotte's favourite Romanian dessert: a sweet leavened bread with raisins which took a long time to make. She'd first tried it a few years ago when Helena had made it for her, and she'd been in love with it ever since.

Helena smiled, 'Yez. I make it just for you because you like.'

Charlotte kissed her on the cheek. 'You're the best. I can't wait to eat it. I just need to check the data again.'

She went to her study and checked the computer. Her program had indexed all the data, listing file names and types, folders, and analysis of words and content. Standard stuff for a teenage boy. Lots of games, lots of instant messaging chat. Not much else.

She typed 'David' in the search field.

The results appeared on the screen. There were a couple of conversations with that name on the Discord chat, and on one of them Daniel had put a note, 'Tutor Dave'.

'Great,' Charlotte said. But there were no identifying features on the chat, just arrangements to meet.

She picked up the phone and rang Angus. 'Daniel met David every Wednesday at 4.30pm at the coffee shop opposite the Met Office entrance on Honiton Road.'

'I know it. Any other details?'

'Not that I can see. I've done a standard Google search for IT tutors working in the area called David, but his name is too common.'

'All right, thanks.'

Charlotte put the phone down and went back to the kitchen. 'Put lunch on hold, I'm going out.'

ANGUS WENT STRAIGHT to the cafe on Honiton Road. It was strategically positioned near the Met Office to get their employees' custom and was impersonal, but popular. You knew you'd get the drink you wanted, and they had all those weird nut and soya milks that people seemed to like, as well as syrups and a never-ending list of coffees. The aroma of toasted sandwiches met his nose the moment he walked in and made his mouth water.

There was a short queue at the counter, and he joined it. He'd get coffee and something to eat and ask questions at the same time.

When he got to the front of the queue, he chose a sandwich and ordered an Americano from the woman behind the till. 'Do you know a man called David who tutors people in here? He's been coming in on Wednesday afternoons, maybe other days too.'

She nodded. 'Yeah, I know who you mean; he comes in here a lot. But why do you want to know?'

'I'm looking for the missing boy, Daniel Cray–you might have seen something about it on Facebook or Insta-gram? I'm helping his parents find him. I think David might know something about where Daniel is.'

'I saw a post about that on Facebook,' she said. 'I don't know the family myself, but my daughter Ellie does. That's him, over there.' She indicated to the left side of the seating area.

Angus took his coffee and headed towards the man. He sat with a laptop open, typing. His hair was brown with a hint of grey and he wore a fading black T-shirt and jeans. He looked as if he'd last shaved a few days ago.

'David?'

The man looked up. 'Yes?'

Angus sat down opposite him without asking if he could join him. David eyed him suspiciously.

'My name is Angus Darrow. I'm helping Daniel Cray's parents find him, he's gone missing. I understand you were tutoring Daniel.'

David gave a curt nod. 'Yes, that's right. Every Wednesday at four thirty.'

'Why were you tutoring him?'

David's eyebrows rose briefly. 'That's a bit of a stupid question.'

'Indulge me.' Angus pushed up his glasses. He was going to be like that, was he?

'He was struggling with his college course; he'd fallen behind and I helped him get up to speed because he is quite far behind, actually.'

'Do you know where Daniel was getting the money to pay for your tuition?'

David shrugged. 'I don't ask, and it's none of my business,' he said flatly.

'Did Daniel say anything to you that might help his parents find where he is?'

David briefly made eye contact then looked away. 'Not that I can think of. We didn't chat about anything like that. He hired me to help him study. He didn't mention his personal life, only his course.'

Something caught Angus's eye—or rather, someone. He stared for a moment as Charlotte Lockwood sat down a few tables away. Her hair neatly styled, showed off her carefully makeup face. She wore navy trousers and a bottle green sweater. What's she doing here?

She didn't make eye contact, but smiled; this was no coincidence. She opened her laptop and started typing, and a moment later, his phone pinged.

'Excuse me,' he said to David. He read the message. *Keep him talking until I leave.*

Angus put his phone away. What is she doing? 'Er, did Daniel book you for a lesson this week?'

'Yes, he did. He said he found the lessons helpful and wanted them for the next six or seven weeks at least. He really gave no sign at all that he was running away. And it's very inconvenient that he's gone off without giving me any notice; I could have used his hour to work with someone else. I don't think he'll pass if he doesn't come back, and all his hard work will be in vain.'

'How did you hear he was missing?'

David shrugged. 'It's all over social media.'

Angus nodded and took a sip of coffee. Then covertly noticed Charlotte was still typing, and he'd nearly exhausted his questions. How long did she need to do whatever she was doing?

'Did Daniel talk about a job or his career plans after the course? University, perhaps?'

He shook his head. 'I'm sorry. He only talked about his course: that he was behind and needed help. I don't chat to my tutees or offer personal support, I just tutor them.'

'Why do you think he was behind with his course? His college principal said his grades were good.'

'That's because I helped him. He was interested in the course, but got distracted by playing games or chatting online. Like many teenagers, his parents had no idea what he was doing in his bedroom, and it wasn't studying.' He looked at his watch and pushed his chair back. 'I've got to go. I've a bus to catch.'

Out of the corner of his eye, Angus saw Charlotte close her laptop, finish her espresso and get up. Perfect timing.

He reached into his pocket and took out a card. 'If you think of anything else that might help me find Daniel, or if he contacts you, please call me straight away.'

David took the card and read it. 'I will.'

As soon as he could, Angus left the cafe and looked for Charlotte. She was nowhere to be seen. He tried to call her, but it went straight to voicemail. He got in his car and as he started it, a text message came back:

At your house.

He found her waiting outside. Her Bentley parked on the street. 'What are you doing here? And how do you know where I live?'

'It's nice to see you too, Mr Darrow,' she replied in her politest voice.

'What were you doing in the cafe?' he asked more gently.

'Can we go inside?'

Angus assessed her for a moment. 'Sure.' He gestured towards the house, and they went in.

She followed him into the kitchen diner and he put the kettle on, not bothering to ask her if she wanted a drink. 'I was hacking–I mean looking–to see what I could get off David's computer. That was David the tutor, wasn't it?'

He nodded. 'Find anything?'

She frowned. 'Annoyingly, no. He used a VPN–a Virtual Private Network. It's a secure link, all encrypted, and unhackable. Well, not totally, but it takes a very long time to hack.' She paused for a moment. 'But then again, he's an IT tutor, so he'd know that using a public network in a cafe is a bad idea. Anyone like me could see exactly what he was doing.'

'I have no idea what you're talking about. Again.' He rubbed the back of his neck.

Charlotte took that as a prompt that he wanted to know more. 'If you use public Wi-Fi in a cafe or similar, anyone can read what you're doing if they're using it too. Most people don't know how, but it's easy to download software. That's what a VPN does: it encrypts everything you do, so people like me can't see.'

'Is it legal to tap into people's messages?' Angus poured milk into the cups.

Charlotte just smiled. After a pause, she asked, 'Did he tell you anything about Daniel?'

'Not really. He wasn't any help at all.'

'That's disappointing.'

'Indeed.'

'What next then, Angus Darrow?'

Angus shook his head. 'You don't have to worry about that.'

Charlotte looked down and frowned.'I want to help. What's wrong? Don't you need my help?'

'I'm not sure how many favours you owe Woody, but I can't afford to pay you.'

'I don't need money; I have plenty of my own. Besides, my therapist said I should find something to focus on to help me get over my bastard ex-husband cheating on me. This could be it.' He handed her the mug and she took a sip.

He stared at her for a moment, processing what she'd said, then sighed and rubbed the bridge of his nose. 'OK, in that case I need help to track down his online friends. On the contact list you gave me everyone has stupid nicknames or whatever you call them, and I can't work out who's who. It seems he had friends all around the country and I don't know who they are.'

'OK, I'll get on it. Have you still got his laptop?'

'Yes, it's in the other room.'

A knock at the door interrupted them. 'That will be Helena, she said she was dropping by.'

Angus opened the door and watched as Helena swept in and they kissed each other on the cheek.

'My love, we've had a change of plan,' said Charlotte. 'I'm not going to the spa this evening. I've got some work to do here.'

Helena put her hands on her hips. 'But you need spa, sauna, hot tub. You grumpy bitch, you need relax.'

'I'm working on finding this missing boy. You go. Take a friend and we can go next week.'

'But you love spa!'

'I know, but I really want to work on this. Take your friend, Oana.'

'Charlotte go crazy. Menopause.' Helena explained to Angus.

Charlotte sighed. 'I am still here, you know. And some of it's menopause but it's mainly my ex-husband.'

'He bastard.' Helena told Angus, putting extra emphasis on the last word.

Charlotte nodded. 'He is.'

Angus said nothing, his attention drawn to the car waiting in front of the house. The Bentley he'd seen parked earlier now had a uniformed driver sat in the front. He must have been there before. Charlotte really must have a lot of money.

'All right I go spa, take Oana.' Helena turned to Angus. 'You make sure she eat. No vodka, whisky or any alcohol. When she drink she sleep with man. And no sex with her OK?' She wagged her finger at him.

'OK,' he replied, holding up his hands in surrender.

Charlotte's eyes met Angus's. 'Sorry,' she mouthed, and his lips twitched in amusement.

When Helena left, Angus retrieved the laptop and handed it to Charlotte. 'Thanks. I'll work in there,' she didn't wait for him to respond, but walked through to the lounge and plonked herself on the sofa.

He followed her through, not sure whether he was

annoyed or just shocked she just made herself at home without having a conversation about it first. She was either rude or maybe on the autistic spectrum like Daniel.

'How long do you think it will take?' He asked.

'Couple of hours at least.' She started tapping at the keyboard.

'Have you had some lunch - would you like something?' He asked.

'That would be lovely - thank you.'

He nodded, then left the room.

After a few hours of intense work, Charlotte had made a list of the friends in a spreadsheet. She took it to Angus. 'This is their name, this is their IP address and this is their probable identity.'

'Probable?'

'Well, their IP address is only their last location. Some of them are unlisted so I can only guess who they are.'

'IP address… Is that the location address of the network they're on?'

'That's right,' said Charlotte, shooting him an approving look. 'Not such the technophobe after all.'

'I've picked a few things up on the way, but not much.'

'Well in that case, you'll know that someone's IP address can change depending on their physical location. So if they're using a laptop or a mobile device, it's hard to know who they are if they travel around a lot. Luckily, most of Daniel's online friends were fairly static.'

Angus scanned the list. Ten people, and she'd identified eight of them. Two in Scotland, three in London, one in Taunton and the other two somewhere in south-east England.

'Where I can, I've identified who they are, but it's tricky; the IP address can only give you an approximate location. I'm working on getting more information about them and I'll let you know when I find more.'

Angus nodded, 'Good work.'

Charlotte didn't pause for breath before continuing. 'I know. The only thing is, I can't tie any of them to the email message Daniel received.'

'What do you mean?'

'Every email sent has the sender's IP address hidden until you delve deeper. But that IP address doesn't match any of his friends'. I'll have to hack into the email account it came from.'

Angus sighed.

'What?' She stared at him.

Angus folded his arms across his chest and stared back. 'Just don't tell me when you are doing something illegal, OK?'

'A vulnerable boy has been sextorted and I'm trying to hack into the baddie's email and *I'm* the one in the wrong?'

Angus raised an eyebrow. 'Baddies?'

'Don't laugh. Please.'

But he couldn't suppress a smile. 'I suppose it is accurate, but in the police we call them suspects.'

'Boring. I prefer baddies.'

He shook his head and chuckled. 'I've got to go, I'm meeting someone. You'll need to go too.'

'Is it to do with the case? Can I come?'

He shook his head. 'He's an old colleague and he'll be more forthcoming if I go on my own.'

She shrugged. 'Oh well, I've got a friend coming over anyway.' Charlotte called a taxi and left after she made Angus promise he'd update her with any new information.

Chapter 11

Angus had texted his old sergeant, Simon Pearce, earlier and Simon had been keen to meet up rather than speak on the phone. Pearce had been Angus's sergeant for nearly six years before he left the police. He was competent, eager to please, and dedicated himself to the job, working long hours and putting in extra effort and time even when it wasn't needed.

They met at The Boat Inn, next to the Old Customs House on Exeter Quay. Regeneration had made the quayside an appealing place for tourists and locals. Unique independent shops, an antique centre and many cafes and restaurants drew people in from far and wide. The river Exe was teeming with canoes, kayaks and other small boats, all of which could be hired for a few hours or all day.

The tables outside the inn gave a beautiful view of the river, and the sky was clear and the sun shone brightly. They got their drinks—half a pint of a local ale for Angus, a pint of lager for Simon—and sat outside despite it being

November. The weather was mild and the sun shone brightly warming the late afternoon.

'It's good to see you, sir.' Simon took a sip from his pint. He appeared older than his thirty-five years, with a light splattering of grey in his brown hair. But that was the case with a lot of detectives–the constant pressure of the job made many age prematurely.

'You don't need to call me sir anymore,' Angus said. 'Call me Angus.'

Simon grinned. 'Old habits die hard. It feels weird calling you by your first name.'

'You still not taken the Inspector's exam?' Angus asked, ignoring the comment.

'Not yet; maybe in a few years. How's life on the outside, anyway?'

'Good. I don't miss you lot at all,' Angus said, smiling.

Simon laughed. 'What, not even Chief Constable Broadbent?'

'I miss his excellent motivation and morale-building.' Angus said, deadpan. Most of Devon and Cornwall Police despised Broadbent, and he'd been rapidly promoted as an easy way to make him someone else's problem. How he'd made Chief Constable nobody knew.

'So, what can I help you with?' Simon asked. He was always straight to the point.

'What's the latest on gangs in the area? I'm particularly interested in any operating trafficked or low-paid workers.'

'Not much going on at the moment. There was a gang in South Devon not so long ago using trafficked workers in a holiday park to clean out the caravans and making them live ten to a van. Mostly Eastern Europeans duped into coming over.'

'Nothing else here in Exeter or nearby?' Angus asked.

'The problem is finding out about them; there are so many isolated rural areas. I'm sure several are operating, especially with drugs now that the students are back at university.'

Angus shook his head. 'Everything always picks up when the students go back.'

'Thank goodness for the students: they keep us busy.' Simon leaned forward. 'So what are you working on? I heard you were a bona-fide private investigator now.'

'Usually it's married people who suspect their other half is having an affair. This time, though, it's a vulnerable young adult gone missing.'

'Which one?'

'Daniel Cray.'

Simon frowned. 'I've not seen that report.'

'That's because Missing Persons won't look into it. He left a note, but I've discovered they have blackmailed him into leaving home. Sextortion.'

'What did he do? Video himself shagging a pillow or something?' Simon laughed, then stopped when he saw Angus's serious face.

'Pretty much. He's autistic. They told him to leave home and he's not been seen since.'

'How did you find this out?'

'His computer.'

Simon stared at him, mouth open. 'You must have had help. You always hated technology.'

'I still do. And yes, I have help. Woody's sister. Turns out she's a computer genius.'

Simon continued to stare. 'Woody's sister?'

'Yep.'

'Are you sure?'

'Yeah. Why?'

'She's totally minted. Like, a multi-millionaire.' He

paused and examined Angus's reaction of a slow disbelieving shake of his head 'He didn't tell you that?'

'No. I mean, it's obvious that she's not poor.'

Simon carried on, happy to help explain. 'She owned this tech company. Cyber security. Sold it about eighteen months ago for £200 million.'

Angus nearly spat out his ale. '£200 million?'

'Yep.'

'Shit.'

'I know. Her husband owned half; they started the business together. But here's the thing: as soon as the sale went through, he left her and shacked up with her best friend.'

'That explains so much.'

'Really? Tell me more. What's she like?'

Angus thought for a moment. 'I've only just met her this morning, so I can't say much. But she seems a little unpredictable.' Angus recalled how she'd been hungover, spent the night with a man whose name she couldn't remember. Angus was no psychoanalyst, but she was clearly trying to get over her husband leaving by sleeping with lots of men. He wouldn't tell Simon though. Friends and ex-colleagues would talk about the sex lives of women they knew—usually women they'd had sex with – always with a side-order of boasting, but Angus thought it indelicate to talk about such things. What Charlotte did in her private life was up to her.

Simon took a sip of beer. 'I'm not surprised. Having your partner and best friend go off together can't be easy. It's going to give you trust issues.'

'At the very least.'

Simon raised his eyebrows. 'So why's she helping you then? Has she run out of money?'

Angus shook his head. 'She's still got plenty from what

I've seen. I'm not paying her; I can't afford to. Woody said she owed him a few favours.'

'Splash the cash, does she?'

'I have no idea, but she has a big house in Topsham – the nice bit – and a Bentley with a driver and a housekeeper.'

Simon whistled. 'There isn't a bad bit of Topsham.'

'Exactly.'

'Get in there if you can.' He winked.

Angus shook his head and stared out across the river. A rich and attractive woman like Charlotte would have many men after her. He wasn't interested in pursuing a woman just because she was loaded. He did like her though. She was plain talking - he liked that.

Simon set his glass down. 'Anyway, your case. There's a suspected gang operating in the Sowton area. They're based at the closed-down DIY store, the one next to the carpet shop. This is really new info; it could be nothing.'

'Are they being monitored?'

'Not yet. We're all busy with other stuff, but we should have resources in about a week or so. They might have moved by then, but there's not much we can do. You know how it is.'

'I've got one last favour to ask. Is there any chance I can get access to the CCTV on the day he went missing?'

'I don't see why not, although it'll have to be unofficial, of course. The council control the cameras but it's still easy to get them to send the recordings. Which areas did you want to look at?'

'Anything around Northernhay Gardens, Rougemount and the high street?'

'Leave it to me.'

'Thanks, Simon.'

Chapter 12

The information from Simon was helpful, though, of course it might have nothing to do with Daniel. But he decided he had to look into it, so he searched the location and went straight there. He parked up at a suitable distance and watched.

The building was in Sowton, an area south of the city known for its excessive amount of business parks. Most of the buildings in this section were occupied, but a few, like this one, had stood empty for long periods of time. It was a brick building with a row of five separate units, each with a large garage door and an entrance door on the right. The one Simon had mentioned was on the end.

He'd been waiting nearly half an hour when a white van pulled up. A man in scruffy jeans and T-shirt got out, went to the passenger side of the van, dragged out a young man and led him inside the building.

This definitely warranted closer scrutiny. Angus wrote down the van's registration number and details in his note-book. An hour later, with no further movement in or out of the building, Angus went home. He'd love to get inside the building and see what was going on, but he'd need a very good reason.

At eight thirty, he was back home and watching the football, eating dinner. His phone pinged. A text from Charlotte: *Come over, I need to see you.*

He yawned and replied:

Can it wait until tomorrow?

A minute later: *No, I need to see you.*

What is it?

I'll explain when you get here. C xxxxx

I was about to go to bed.

It's really early. Come on, I really need to see you.

He really was about to go to bed, as he was planning a longer early-morning run: a 10K. He'd been trying to improve his 5K time, and had read that running a longer distance was supposed to help. He picked up the phone again.

Are you sure it can't wait until tomorrow?

Yes

He sighed and rubbed his eyes. If he left now, he'd be back before ten.

Twenty minutes later, Angus knocked on Charlotte's front door. He could hear pop music inside. He knocked harder, and shortly afterwards, the door opened.

'Angus!' She held her arms open. She had a glass in one hand and an almost-empty bottle of whiskey in the other. 'You came!'

She'd changed clothes since he'd last seen her. This time she was wearing a knee high navy blue dress with white flowers and her hair was in a loose side pony tail.

'You said you needed to see me.' The pop music and the smell of booze hit him like a brick wall.

'Come in!' she shouted above the music.

As soon as he was inside, she threw her arms around

him and kissed him on the cheek. 'It's so good to see you! Thanks for coming over. Where have you been, you naughty man? I've been waiting for you all night.'

Eventually Charlotte let go of him. Her eyes were glazed, and he suspected she was very, very drunk.

'I've been busy looking for Daniel.' He hated drunk people, and especially drunk women. 'What did you want? Your texts didn't explain.'

She wagged her finger at him. 'Always working, Angus. You need to relax a little; come and have a drink with me. This whiskey is wonderful; it's Irish. I went to the distillery in Dublin a few months back and bought half of the company.' She giggled and held up the bottle.

'I'm not drinking tonight.'

'Boooooring. Just have one, then you can go.'

'Go? You've been texting me to come over. I thought you'd made a breakthrough and I thought you had a friend coming over.' Angus wanted to put his hands over his face in exasperation. She made an over-exaggerated sad face. 'He cancelled.'

'What about the breakthrough?'

'I didn't mention the case. I just wanted to see you. I was lonely.'

'Where's Helena?'

'Home. She doesn't live here you know.'

Angus made a mental note to get Helena's mobile number in case of future emergency - like this. She put the bottle and glass down on the table, then moved closer to him and lowered her voice to a whisper. 'I'm so glad you're here.' She slipped her arms around his neck.

She stared up at him for a few seconds. Her gaze moved from his eyes to his lips and she kissed him full on the mouth.

He stood, unable to move. It had been a long time

since he'd been this close to a woman. Even longer since he'd been intimate with one. Her lips were soft and welcoming. Then he felt her hands move to loosen his tie. She broke off the kiss, 'Are you always so smartly dressed?'

Clarity followed a moment's confusion when he remembered her this morning and the man she'd spent the night with. He stopped her hand with his and pulled away. 'Charlotte, I won't be your next mistake,' he whispered.

'You'd be no one's mistake, Angus.' She put a finger on his chest and focused on it.

'You've had far too much to drink. I'll make you a coffee; I need you focused and capable in the morning, I've got something for you to do.'

'And I've got something for you to do, too.' She kissed him again, just under his ear. Her hands moved down to his backside and he almost jumped away.

'No, Charlotte. Come on, you need to sleep this off.' He took hold of her hands and moved her towards the sofa.

'That's disappointing. Are you sure you don't want to stay the night? I'll be all yours.'

'I'm not having sex with you tonight.'

'Spoilsport.'

'You should go to bed.'

She giggled. 'You'd get me into the bedroom much quicker if you came with me.'

Angus sighed. 'Sit down.' He led Charlotte to the sofa. She sat down and immediately slumped to one side. He went into the kitchen and made coffee, and when he came back into the room, she was asleep.

He found a bedroom, took a duvet and put it over her, then let himself out.

Chapter 13

Outside, he got into his car, put his hands on the steering wheel, tipped his head forwards and gave a seep sigh. Was this day never going to end?

His phone vibrated. What now?

It was Daniel's mother, Mary Cray. 'Mr Darrow?' Her voice was strained.

'Mary, what can I do for you?'

'It's Daniel's Uncle Billy. He's gone missing and there's been reports of a body found on Exmouth beach.'

It took a moment for Angus to process the information. 'What makes you think it's Billy?'

'It's all over social media. The description was of a man similar to Billy, wearing a South West Bus company uniform.'

'Are there any other details?'

'Not really. Janet couldn't get hold of him since last night, but she thought nothing of it at first. He sometimes did that, you know, went off by himself.'

'Thanks for letting me know, Mary. I'll contact my old colleagues and see what I can find out.'

He was close to Exmouth. It was one of Devon's most popular seaside destinations and Charlotte's house was halfway between Exeter and Exmouth; it would only take ten minutes to get there. He started the car and ran through a list of ex-colleagues in the Devon and Cornwall Police, considering which of them owed him a favour. Simon and Woody were the prime candidates still.

It didn't take him long to locate the action, even though the esplanade was 4 miles long. The dark night couldn't hide the cluster of police cars and CSI vans on the east end of the esplanade. November was too late for holidaymakers to be in the town, but there was still a small crowd looking on.

He parked a short distance away, opposite one of the many posh Victorian houses overlooking the sea, and walked up to the police cordon. Behind it were several CSI officers in white hazmat suits.

He regarded the beach below, where a pop-up tent hid the body. He recognised Simon.

He went under the police ribbon and a young officer immediately came over. 'Sorry sir, you're not allowed in.'

'Hello, Fraser, how are you?' said Angus.

Fraser stared at him for a moment, then recognised him. 'Hello sir, it's good to see you. How are you?'

'I'm good thanks, I just need a word with Simon. Is that all right?'

'Of course, sir, go right ahead.'

'Thanks.'

Angus's polished shoes sank in the wet sand, and he cursed to himself. He made a mental note to put some sturdy shoes in his car boot in the future, just in case.

'Simon?'

Simon's back was turned and he was talking to a man

in a white hazmat suit. He turned around when he heard his name.

'Angus, I didn't expect to see you again so soon.' Simon shook his hand. 'What are you doing here? Is this connected to your missing boy?'

'It's possible it's his Uncle Billy.'

Simon pulled the tent curtain aside and they stepped in. Angus looked at the face. 'Yes, that's him.' He recognised the man he'd met briefly in Mary Cray's kitchen yesterday.

It didn't matter how many times he saw a murder victim or a dead body, it always freaked him out a bit. Sad that he'd only met this man the day before.

'They shot him in the side of the head, execution style. Someone wanted him silenced. If his nephew's missing, it might be connected.'

'This is too much of a coincidence.' Angus shook his head.

They stepped outside the tent. 'I'll keep you updated with anything I find,' Simon said.

Angus walked back to his car. He missed crime scene investigation. The paperwork and red tape, though, he didn't miss at all.

This changes everything, he thought. A missing boy, and his uncle now dead. Only a fool would think they weren't connected.

THE FOLLOWING MORNING, Charlotte woke up dazed and confused. She checked the time: 5.30am and wondered where she was, then as the hangover hit her, remembered she'd been drinking again. She'd promised her therapist she'd stop for two months and cursed her lack of self-control. Again.

Her head pounded; she needed water desperately. Realising she was in the lounge, she got up, taking the duvet with her, went to the kitchen and drank a couple of glasses of water, then went to her bedroom and fell asleep again.

At eight o'clock, there was a loud knock on the front door and then the doorbell rang.

Endlessly.

It wouldn't stop.

Someone came in. It must be Helena.

She didn't move. She couldn't move. Her head felt as if it would fall off. She hoped it would; then the hangover would stop.

A deep male voice spoke and she jumped. 'Charlotte, I need you to get up and come with me. I've got a lead on the case and something important has happened.'

She looked up. Angus was standing in her bedroom doorway dressed in a navy check suit, white shirt. This time, no tie. 'Go away,' she croaked, hiding her head under her duvet.

'That's not very nice. You were begging me to come over last night and didn't want me to leave.'

She poked her face over the top of the duvet and stared at him. 'Did I?'

'You don't remember?' He came in and stood by the bed.

'No.'

'I can't go away; I need your help. Be ready in fifteen minutes. And get your equipment ready: whatever you use to hack into people's Wi-Fis.'

'How did you get in?'

'I took the spare set of keys. You were blind drunk last

night, so I wanted to make sure you were all right this morning.' He closed the bedroom door behind him.

Charlotte felt like crying, and not at Angus's thoughtfulness. If she got up, she was sure she'd faint.

Ten minutes later, he knocked on the bedroom door and opened it a crack to speak through. 'Charlotte, come on. I've got important news about the case and I really need you to come out with me. There's a gang working in the area and I need you to hack into their Wi-Fi.'

'That's illegal.'

'I won't tell if you don't. Besides, they're a bunch of criminals. They're hardly going to report you if they find out, which they won't.'

She sat up in bed. 'I need a head transplant.'

'Get in the shower. I've brought you my hangover cure; you can have it after you've dressed. I'll be in the kitchen.'

Twenty minutes later, Charlotte stood in the kitchen, her hair wet she'd put on a pair of jeans and a black blouse. 'Sit down.' He indicated the stool. 'Drink this.' He handed her a glass.

She examined it and her nose wrinkled. 'It's green.'

'It is. It's also the best hangover cure this side of the Exe.'

'What's in it? Swamp water?'

He chuckled. 'It's not swamp water. It's a secret, but nothing disgusting. Lots of healthy minerals and electrolytes to reset your body.'

'Electrowhats?'

'Just drink it. Trust me, it works.'

Charlotte took a sip, then found a couple of painkillers and washed them down with the rest of the swamp water. 'Tastes better than it looks.' She drained the glass.

'Give it about twenty minutes, you'll feel ten years younger.'

'So what is the news?' she asked, thumping the empty glass on the counter and wincing.

'Daniel's uncle. He's been murdered.'

'Really? How?'

Angus told her briefly about his trip to Exmouth the previous night.

Charlotte frowned. 'This has to be connected.'

'I agree.'

'It's most likely a gang behind it. As soon as the pounding in my head stops, I'll start searching on the internet and deep web. Are you going to talk to his wife?'

'Yeah, I'll head over there later. She'll ID his body, but that's just a formality.'

'I never thought Exmouth would have an execution-style murder.' She shook her head. 'Just a few miles away, too.'

Chapter 14

An hour later, they were sitting in Angus's car outside the industrial unit in Sowton.

Charlotte took a sip of the coffee Angus had made her. It was in a travel mug she didn't recognise so it must be his. 'You do great hangover cures and coffee. Remind me why you're single again?'

A small smile curved his lips.

'Oh my God!' she cried. 'Oh my God.' She drew back until she pressed against the car door.

Angus frowned. 'What is it?'

'I made a pass at you last night!'

Angus said nothing.

'Oh my God, I'm so sorry.' She put her hands over her mouth, then covered her eyes. 'Shit, shit, shit. Did I say sorry? I'm a complete fucking mess at the moment and especially when I'm drunk.'

'Maybe you should stop drinking.'

She grimaced. 'I know.'

Silence fell, then Charlotte turned to him with a suspicious expression. 'Hang on a minute. You turned me down!'

Angus stared through the windscreen.

She sighed and sipped her coffee. 'I can't believe you turned me down.' Another pause. 'Are you gay?'

'No,' he replied, with a small laugh.

'It's just that I know lots of gay men who came out when they were older. You know, they've been hiding it for most of their lives but finally come to realise they can't hide their true sexuality anymore. Like Philip Schofield. Married for 27 years with two kids. Is that why you broke up with your wife?'

'No.'

'I mean, it doesn't matter to me if you are. I've got loads of gay friends. Well, three–that's quite a lot. And there's also Gary, he used to work for me. He's married, and I think internal homophobia's stopping him from coming out. Plus, he's really religious. I've seen him staring at a male colleague more than once. A sort of wistful, lustful look.'

She turned to look at him and took another sip of coffee. 'Well?'

'I'm *not* gay.' This time he looked at her.

'Just wondered why you passed on the opportunity of no-strings sex. Guess you're not attracted to me, then.'

He turned back to the windscreen.

She examined his profile. She didn't think he was gay. She had good gaydar. Usually.

'Helena will not be happy with me when I tell her. She'll be happy with you, though, for turning me down. She thinks I sleep around far too much. My therapist, Misty, will scold me, too. She told me not to make a pass at you and keep it platonic.'

That made him turn to her with a frown. 'You've been

talking about me to your therapist? And her name is Misty? I've only known you a bit more than 24 hours.'

'I talk to her about everything. I phone her a lot lately. Don't worry, I didn't tell her the exact details of what we're working on, just that you needed my help with something. Everything is strictly confidential anyway, but I won't tell her. She's just helping me come to terms with my bastard husband and best friend going off together. Trying to make sure I don't go off the rails.'

'I'm not sure it's working. How much are you paying her?'

'Ouch. I was much worse than I am now, you know. She reckons I've been having sex with lots of men to punish myself, and to prove to my subconscious that I'm still attractive after being rejected by my husband.' She took another sip of coffee. 'I'm not sure, though. I have noticed since the peri-menopause started that I want sex a lot more. Being able to have sex with little or no worry about getting pregnant is quite liberating. Did you notice that with your ex-wife?'

'No.'

'Maybe she's different.'

'She certainly is.'

'And you're not gay?'

He gave her a withering glance.

'Sorry, it's just that I've never been turned down before.' She pondered for a moment. 'It's quite a novelty, actually. Is that what it's like to be a man? You want sex all the time, but you get turned down.'

'That's exactly what it's like,' he said with a chuckle.

'Harsh.'

'You learn to live with it.'

'That might take some getting used to.'

'Indeed.'

Charlotte looked at the building outside. 'So, what are we doing here?' she asked deliberately, changing the subject.

'I need you to do your juju with the computer and see if you can work out what they are up to in there. The same thing you did in the cafe.'

'All right.' She opened her laptop and about ten minutes later she closed it. 'There's no network. Whatever they're up to, they're using mobile phones to do it.'

'That's disappointing.' Angus said. 'Can you hack mobile signals?'

'I'd have to hack the base station, and that's risky. If I get caught, it's a long prison sentence. The encryption they use is hard to crack too: bit-streaming encryption. It's almost uncrackable.'

'OK, I'll try something else. I just want to know what's going on. I think they may have kidnapped a boy. I saw him dragged into here last night.'

'Really? That's awful.' A moment later, Charlotte got out of the car and started walking towards the building.

Angus caught up with her. 'What are you doing?'

'I'm going in.'

'No you're not.' He grabbed her arm.

She turned to him. 'I've got an idea.'

'Charlotte, a dangerous gang could be working in there. You can't go in.'

'Relax, I know what I'm doing.'

'No you don't.'

They stared at each other for a moment.

'I'm going in now or I'll come back later on my own.' Charlotte shook her arm free.

'You're insufferable.'

'I just want to find Daniel.'

She hurried to the front door and tried the handle. It was unlocked, and she went in.

It opened into a long corridor, with many doors on the right-hand side and one at the end. Charlotte stopped outside the first and peered through the small window. An office with white walls, a desk and chairs and several large cardboard boxes. She couldn't see anyone, so tried the door. Angus was right behind her.

No-one was there. On the desk were empty drink cans and food packets.

'Someone's been sleeping on the floor.' Angus pointed to a sleeping bag and a small pile of clothes in the corner.

Charlotte delved into her handbag, pulled out a Swiss army knife and used it to open one of the cardboard boxes.'Sombreros?' She lifted one out. 'I wasn't expecting that.'

She opened another box. 'Harry Potter lunch boxes…' She unzipped one. 'Nothing inside.'

Angus pulled a few more out and felt in the bottom of the box. 'Nothing.'

'You thought there might be drugs?'

'Yes.' He glanced at the other boxes.

'Let's see what else is here,' said Charlotte.'Come on, we might as well.' She went towards the door, but it opened before she reached it and she froze.

'Who are you?' A teenage boy wearing jeans and a dark-blue T-shirt stood in the doorway. It was the young man Angus had seen the night before being dragged into the building.

Chapter 15

'Are you Mick? Come for my dad?' The boy asked.

Angus, who'd been standing behind a pile of boxes, came forward. 'Does your dad own the white van outside?'

'Yeah, that's his.'

'So you work for your dad here?' said Angus, playing for time.

'Yeah. Who are you?'

Charlotte stepped forward. 'We're from the planning department at the council; we've come to check the building regulations and need to make sure everything is correct now that the building is in use again.'

'What's building regulations?' he asked, looking from one to the other.

'You know, making sure all the rooms conform to the original plan and there haven't been any unlawful changes. We just need to check that the other rooms are as they should be and then we'll be on our way.'

'Oh, OK.' His eyes darted from one to the other.

'How long have you been here?' Angus asked.

'Couple of weeks.'

'Is your father around?'

'He's popped out, he'll be back in about half an hour. You can wait for him if you like.'

'No need. It won't take long and then we'll be out of your way.' She gave him a tight smile and glanced at Angus's pained expression. Charlotte walked out of the room and down the corridor. The next room was the toilet. It smelt of urine but was otherwise empty. After that came a large workshop with a small sink on one side, almost empty but for a few more cardboard boxes.

'What is it you do here?' Angus asked the boy, who had followed them.

'Dad sells stuff on eBay. Goes like hot cakes.' He grinned.

'What sort of stuff?'

'Mugs, lunch boxes, that sort of stuff. Mostly tat but it sells well. Pet memorials are our best seller,' he said proudly.

'And sombreros?' Charlotte commented.

He took one out of the box and put it on. He looked ridiculous.

'And you help your dad?' she continued.

'Yeah. I pack the orders and take them to the couriers.'

'Well, that all seems in order. We can tick everything off and leave you alone now.' Charlotte said.

They were heading for the door when it opened and a small figure came in: a teenager, dressed in jeans and a pulled-up hoody.

She stopped as soon as she saw Angus and Charlotte, then glanced at the boy.

'All right?' he said to her.

'Who are they?' she demanded.

'They're from the council.'

'Planning.' said Charlotte. 'And everything is in order,

so we're just heading off…'

She walked to the door, but Angus didn't move. 'Isabelle, you've got the police searching for you and your parents are worried sick.'

The girl's eyes widened and she glanced at the door.

Angus took a step forward. 'You need to go home.'

'I'm not going back,' she muttered, then made a break for the door.

'Run, Belle, run!' The boy shouted.

'Stay here,' said Angus, and he ran after the girl.

'What is she doing here?' Charlotte asked the boy.

'We just want to be together.' The boy stuck his chin out. 'Her parents don't approve of me. Don't think I'm good enough.'

If I had a daughter, I wouldn't approve of you either, thought Charlotte. 'So she's been staying with you?'

'Yeah, my dad don't know. Don't tell him, he'll kill me.'

That explained the sleeping bag. 'I can't promise anything,' said Charlotte. Then again, his dad would probably kill her too, for pretending to be from the council.

A few moments later, Angus came in holding Isabelle, who was wriggling and flailing to no avail. He let her go and stood in the doorway, blocking it. 'There are a lot of people searching for you.'

'I don't want to go home.' She moved next to the boy and they held each other.

'You have to,' said Charlotte. 'You're sixteen and you can't leave home without your parents' consent.'

'If they cared about me, they wouldn't ban me from seeing him.'

Angus pulled his phone out and dialled. After a few moments, he turned away and spoke in a hushed tone. Five minutes later, three police officers arrived and took Isabelle home. Angus and Charlotte made a fast retreat.

Back at Angus's house, they sat drinking tea.

'If that girl just ran away for love,' said Charlotte, 'that means she's not involved with the gang.'

'It seems so,' said Angus. 'At least, not in any significant way.'

'Very Romeo and Juliet, running away from disapproving parents. In a few years, she'll wonder what she saw in him.'

'Are you speaking from experience?'

She glanced at him over her cup. 'He was called Dave and he was in the year above me at school. He got himself arrested for fighting with his father, and my parents banned him as a boyfriend. Overall, a lucky escape. So the gang isn't a gang, just someone selling tat over the internet. What next?'

'I need to visit Janet to talk about her husband's murder.'

'While you do that, I can hack her computer and see what I find,' Charlotte offered.

Angus rolled his eyes. 'Is that your answer to everything? Hack someone's computer?'

'It can reveal so much about a person. As I'm sure you know.'

'Depends what the crime was. In the early days, most people didn't realise that even if they deleted the content, it was still there on the hard drive. A few years later, they'd worked that out.' Angus glanced at his watch. 'It's lunchtime. Want something to eat?'

'Yes, please. I need some food; your hangover cure is wearing off. What's in it again?'

Angus smiled. 'I told you, it's a secret.' He stood up and went to the bread bin.

'I want to come with you to see Janet.' Charlotte said, watching him cut bread rolls and butter them.

'You're better off staying here and doing your juju on the computer.' He went to the fridge for cheese. 'We still need to look into Daniel's online friends.'

'I'm already doing that. I set off search botnets.'

Angus stared at her. 'Whatnets?'

Charlotte laughed. 'A botnet. It's an automated search program I wrote years ago. It does all the work of searching the internet and dark web for me; all I have to do is set it running. I tweak it every now and again but it's rather an excellent piece of code, even if I say so myself. You didn't think I searched things manually, did you?'

'I didn't know what you did.'

'Clearly. You really need to get your IT skills up to scratch; most people our age have much better computer skills than you. Didn't they give you any training when you were in the police?'

'I always turned it down. And I'd rather you didn't come.' He cut precise slices of tomato and placed them on the cheese.

'That isn't very polite.' She tried to ignore the feeling of rejection that went through her.

'I prefer to work alone when I interview people.'

'I bet you didn't work alone in the police.'

He gave her a sidelong look. 'You don't have any experience in interviewing people.'

'No, but I can learn from a pro.'

'Flattery, now, is it?' He put her sandwich on a plate and handed it to her.

'Just stating a fact,' she replied nonchalantly. 'I promise to let you do the talking. I'll simply be there to take notes and learn.'

'I suppose having a woman there might make her feel more at ease.'

'Great!' She took a bite of the sandwich.

Chapter 16

An hour later, Charlotte was sitting next to Angus in Janet's lounge. She lived in Heavitree, in a Victorian terraced house similar to Daniel's and only a few streets away.

That was the only thing that was similar, though. Inside, the house looked as though no one had bothered to redecorate for years: a worn, faded carpet that should have been replaced years ago, and walls with cracks in them. At least the three-piece suite in the lounge had covers on which hid its true state.

The house was the exact opposite to Janet, who looked as smart as before. She wore a smart flowery knee-length dress with black leggings underneath, her short pixie-cut hair was styled into a quiff, and her face was immaculately made up despite being newly widowed.

'I'm sorry for your loss.' Angus said in a serious tone, 'Thank you for seeing us, especially so quickly. I appreciate that this is a difficult time for you but we need to find Daniel. It's even more important now.'

Janet, hunched on the edge of her seat, nodded and

dabbed her eyes with a tissue, even though there didn't seem to be anything to mop up.

Charlotte glanced at the door, wondering if she should offer to make tea, but she didn't want to miss the conversation. She might offer in a minute; while she was in the kitchen, she could easily hack the Wi-Fi and leave a worm virus to send her information. If Janet's husband Billy had been doing anything dodgy, there would be an electronic trail on the computer.

'How long were you married?' Angus asked.

'Twenty-six years.'

'Do you have kids?'

'No: we decided not to. Well, Billy didn't want any, and I wasn't bothered. We loved Daniel, though, and looked after him a lot, especially when he was little.'

Angus took out his notebook and pen. 'I realise the police will have asked you this, but when did you last see him?'

'Last night, at about eight. He said he was going out to meet friends at the pub.'

'Was this something he did regularly?'

'Yes. Not usually on a Monday, but he'd go out at least two or three times a week to meet friends. Not always at the pub. We'd been spending all our time outside work looking for Daniel, and we needed some time away from it.' She paused. 'But the friends he usually meets at the pub said he didn't come that night that night, so he was lying.' She crossed her arms and sat back in the chair.

'Did his friends have any idea where he'd gone?'

She shook her head.

Charlotte glanced at Angus, wondering if he had the same suspicion as her: that Billy could have been seeing another woman. She didn't catch his eye.

'He said Daniel missing was his fault. He always looked

out for Daniel, like any uncle would, so I thought that was what he meant.' She frowned. 'I thought when they found him, he'd killed himself. He went through a difficult time a few years ago. His mental health wasn't great back then, but he came through it and after he said he'd considered about killing himself. Do you think his murder is connected to Daniel going missing?'

'It's possible. It would help us know if he'd said anything else to you.'

'Nothing different from what I've already told you. He was just an ordinary bloke, you know. Not that much going on other than work and meeting his friends in the pub.'

'Can you think of any reason why someone would want him dead?'

She dabbed her eyes. 'Maybe. I mean, I tried to help him when he had problems but in the end, I couldn't deal it anymore.'

'What sort of problems? Mental health?' Charlotte asked in a concerned voice.

'Gambling. He couldn't stop, he went to Gamblers Anonymous, but always went back to his old ways. He tried and tried but it was no good. It started with the odd flutter down the bookie, then it didn't take him long to find a private poker club. That's why he got depressed. He got into debt - borrowed a lot of money. In the end, he managed to pay it all off, but I never found out how. He just said he sorted it. I figured it was better not to ask any questions.'

There was a long silence until Charlotte's gentle voice broke it. 'Was there anyone who had a problem with him? Someone he lost money to or argued with?'

Janet looked up. 'I don't know of anyone. He got on with most people. He liked to be popular.'

Charlotte remembered she was supposed to be hacking the Wi-Fi. She stood up. 'Can I use your loo?'

Janet nodded. 'Upstairs, first room on the left.'

As soon as she was in the bathroom, Charlotte took out her phone and launched her Wi-Fi App. She waited for it to scan and report. She looked around her. The room was tiny. The bath had piles of clothes in it, and the area around the sink was loaded with makeup and creams. Her phone pinged. The app had finished the scan. No Wi-Fi's close by, only two or three in the neighbouring houses. That couldn't be right. There was always Wi-Fi. She tried the app again and got the same result.

Charlotte sighed admitting defeat and went back downstairs.

When she entered the living room, Angus and Janet were silent.

'I'm sorry about the mess up there. I clean people's clothes as a side-hustle and what with Billy, I've got a bit behind. The toilet flushed ok? It's a bit temperamental. Billy said he was going to fix it but he never did.'

'Er, it was fine. No problem.' Angus stood up and gave Charlotte a resigned look. 'Thank you for giving us your time, especially under the circumstances. If you think of anything, however insignificant, let us know.'

Outside, they got into Angus's car and looked at each other. 'What do you think?' Charlotte asked. 'Do you think she's lying?'

'I don't think she's lying about knowing about Daniel, but she's definitely hiding something.'

'Gut feeling?'

'Yes. And most of the time my gut is right.' Angus walked to the car and Charlotte followed. 'How did the Wi-Fi hack go?'

'What makes you think I was hacking her Wi-Fi? Maybe I needed to pee.'

Angus raised his eyebrows.

'Alright alright, I went to hack her Wi-Fi, but there wasn't one. Annoying and suspicious.

'There's nothing suspicious about not having Wi-Fi.'

Charlotte put her hands on her hips. 'There definitely is. No Wi-Fi means they could have a wired network and wired networks mean you don't want your Wi-Fi hacked and you might be hiding something.'

'I didn't see a computer, let alone a wired network.'

'I checked the bedrooms upstairs and there wasn't one up there, which meant the kitchen was the only place left. Most people don't have computers in the kitchen.'

'Either way, we need to find Daniel, and quickly. Billy's death was connected. Either he found Daniel or he was involved.

Chapter 17

Back at Angus's house, they went into the kitchen. Charlotte reached into her bag and pulled out her tablet. 'Now that's over, we need to go over the list of Daniel's online friends.'

'Anything interesting?'

'Yes and no.' Charlotte paused, choosing her next words carefully. 'They're certainly different.'

'Sounds ominous.'

'They're all online gamers, and they play a game called Escape from Pirate Island. Daniel's in their team. They talk to each other on a server as they play and they work together to win. They battle against other teams all over the world.'

Angus stared at her. 'People really do this?'

'Yep. It's huge. This is just one of many games that millions of people play all the time.'

'I'll stick to Scrabble.'

'Real life or the app?'

'There's a Scrabble app?' Angus's nose wrinkled. 'I prefer real life.'

'Who do you play Scrabble with?'

'Anyone who is willing? Do you play?'

'Not for years. I used to play with my sons when they were at school to improve their spelling.'

Charlotte put her tablet on the table and called up a photo of a dark-haired, bearded man. 'The first team member is Dave King. Approximately 30, he likes steam engines and works in a food-processing factory. I've not found any evidence he's been in contact with Daniel.'

She swiped to the next photo. 'Ben Wright, 21, works at a takeaway pizza joint and seems to spend all his time either making pizza or playing Escape from Pirate Island. No contact with Daniel there, either.

'This is Neil Fowler. He's eighteen and according to his Twitter bio, he likes downloading anime and 'cute shit'. He's also a heavy weed smoker and he writes novels, but he hasn't been in contact with Daniel.'

'He sounds like a bundle of laughs,' Angus commented. 'Where is he getting the weed from?'

Charlotte shrugged. 'Dunno. There's nothing on his computer to tell me.'

'Nothing on his computer to tell you?' Angus raised his eyebrows. 'I'm not even going to ask how you know that.'

She smiled. 'Best you don't.'

She swiped again to show a headshot of a teenage boy, part of his face was hidden by a hoody. 'This is Nexus678. I couldn't get his real name, but he likes Marvel films, streams his gaming, and seems to earn quite a lot of money from it.'

'How does he get money from streaming his gaming?'

'People pay him; he has a donate button and thousands of people watch him. He's popular, though I'm not sure why, looking at the state of him… He should spend some of his money on a trip to the barber.'

Angus sat back in his chair. 'What a way to earn a living. The world's gone mad.'

Charlotte laughed. 'It's mind-boggling, isn't it?'

'These people need to get a proper job and contribute something to society,' Angus said severely.

Charlotte gave him a small smile. 'He won't be earning any money from his computer for a while; it got a virus which wiped everything. He'll have to re-install it all from scratch.'

'A virus?'

'Yep.' Charlotte grinned.

'Anyone else?' Angus sat forward on his chair.

'One more. Sophie is nineteen, and the only woman in the group. She likes cyberpunk and has a My Fans Only page.

'My Fans Only?'

'It's a pay for access site a bit like Instagram it's used by lots of women use it to sell pictures of themselves to only their fans. Obviously you can guess what sort of pictures they are selling.'

'Now that interests me, and not for the content. If she's selling pictures of herself then wouldn't that be connected to Daniel's sextortion?'

Charlotte shook her head. 'There's no indication that she's had contact with Daniel outside the game, but since he went missing, she's mentioned a local hand car wash a few times and said that she's been looking out for him. But she stopped talking about it yesterday. Besides, lots of young women are using sites like that it's not unusual. But...' Charlotte paused for a moment and found something on her iPad. 'She thinks Daniel is being forced to work in a car wash? Certain enough that she goes several times a day to search for him. They're often used to exploit people aren't they?'

'Amongst other things.' Angus nodded.

'The staff are paid next to nothing; it's a form of modern slavery.'

'Where is she?'

'Taunton.' Charlotte opened her maps app. Angus leaned over to see. '40 minutes up the M5.'

'It might be worth checking out, even if it's just to cross it off. I'll keep monitoring what she says.'

'How did you find all this out, Charlotte? Or shouldn't I ask?'

She smiled. 'I hid a piece of code in a file I sent them. It looked like a graphic of Daniel's poster, but it also had code in it that monitored their computer for evidence they were communicating with Daniel.'

'Is that legal?'

Charlotte blinked twice. 'Of course not. But we're trying to find a missing vulnerable boy duped into working for goodness knows who. He could be dead already.'

'I see.' Angus regarded her. 'You didn't tell me about this, and I definitely don't know that you did it.'

'Did what?' Charlotte replied with a small smile. A moment later, she was serious again. 'We need to consider the hand car wash, though. They could be forcing him to work there.'

Angus shook his head. 'I don't know. They often get reported for having slave labour, but I've never heard of a case. When I was in the police we got loads of reports about car washes, but none of them ever came to anything.'

'Doesn't mean it isn't happening,' said Charlotte.

'I can't see any gang like that trying to recruit local teenagers. They go for foreign nationals looking for a new life, not college students.'

Charlotte went quiet for a short time. Then stood up.'Right, well I've got to go. I'll see you soon.'

When she'd gone, Angus pondered whether the information about the girl in Taunton was worth following up. He emptied the bins, put the washing on and cleaned the bathroom.

Half an hour later, he headed up the M5.

Chapter 18

He found the hand car wash easily and parked in a bay the opposite side of the road and near enough to watch it.

Five men were working on the forecourt, all aged under forty. The car wash stood on the site of an old petrol station, and there was a cabin the men disappeared into when a customer paid. He couldn't see inside; the windows had grilles over them.

Angus surveyed the queue of cars waiting to come in and the price list. A basic wash cost £4.99. At that price, the workers would be lucky to get minimum wage.

Half an hour later, the queue had gone. The men stood around, smoking and chatting, and Angus contemplated going in and asking the men if they'd seen Daniel. Then again, whoever employed the men would keep a close eye on them, probably from the cabin. Even if they knew something, they'd probably keep quiet.

He had just started the engine when he saw a Bentley pull into the car wash.

Charlotte.

Angus swore under his breath.

As soon as the car had stopped moving, the men put out their cigarettes and stared at it.

Her driver, a short, stocky man in a chauffeur's uniform, got out and waddled over to the workers. He said something, and they immediately went to fetch their gear. Then Charlotte got out of the car and walked towards the cabin.

Angus swore again, then swung the car round and drove into the car wash. He parked behind Charlotte's Bentley, then went into the cabin.

Inside, Charlotte was standing in front of a desk, behind which sat a stocky man, shaking his head. They both looked round when Angus came in.

'What are you doing here?' Angus demanded.

Charlotte raised her eyebrows. 'Hello, Angus.' She looked him up and down. 'What am *I* doing here? Well, what do you think I'm doing here? And what are you doing here? I thought you said this wasn't worth pursuing.'

He ignored her question. 'You should have told me you were coming.' She was getting annoying now, and he wasn't sure if it was because she kept appearing everywhere or if it was because he was starting to like her even more.

'Should I? You don't have a monopoly on finding Daniel, you know.'

Angus paused. She was right. But he had been hired to do it. 'I don't think it's a good idea for you to be snooping around here.' He was also worried about the potential dangers from her investigating. If there were criminal gangs, she'd be at risk.

'I'm not snooping around. I'm looking for Daniel, just like you.' Charlotte put her hands on her hips. She kept doing that and it was endearing. Despite that, he pressed on. 'You're not experienced in questioning people.'

'You're going to play that card, are you?'

'It's true though.'

The man behind the desk shifted in his chair and they both turned to look at him. 'Sergio here hasn't seen Daniel, and he doesn't know where he is.' Sergio had a wad of money in his hand, and Angus surmised that it wasn't from washing cars.

'Grigore is asking the men outside whether they've seen anything,' said Charlotte. 'And before you ask, he has experience questioning people.' She turned to the man behind the desk. 'Thank you, Sergio. If you hear anything or see Daniel, there is a reward if it leads to him being found.'

Sergio grunted.

Charlotte left the cabin and Angus followed. Outside, Grigore was still talking to the five car washers.

Charlotte opened the back door of the Bentley and got in. Angus nipped in after her.

'Do come in,' Charlotte said, raising an eyebrow at him.

'You're going to find the girl next, aren't you?'

'Well, I'm in Taunton and she lives here…'

Angus sighed. He'd have to go with her, not only because she might be onto something, but if anything happened to her, Woody would kill him. 'I'll follow you and we can go together. Let me do the talking.'

'You're being overbearing now.'

'I don't care.'

A moment later, Grigore got into the car. He didn't turn around but spoke to Charlotte via the driver's mirror. 'They no seen Daniel.' He spoke with a strong Romanian accent.

'That's disappointing,' said Charlotte. 'I was really hoping he'd be here.'

'Did they have any information on where he might be?'

Angus asked.

'They say they know nothing,' Grigore turned around. 'This man, you vant him out car?'

'It's all right, Grigore, he's about to leave. By the way, Grigore, this is Angus. Angus, this is Grigore.'

The two men nodded at each other, and Grigore narrowed his beady eyes. Both silently acknowledged that Angus wouldn't stand a chance against him. Grigore looked like he could take on a Grisly Bear and win. At least with Grigore in tow, Charlotte was less at risk. So maybe he was just annoyed she was taking over. He was the ex-policeman with years of experience. She might be a computer whizz, but it didn't mean she could find a missing boy.

'Do you think they're lying?' Charlotte asked Grigore pulling Angus from his thoughts.

'Possible, but most leaving car vash soon to vork in factory. Better pay, no need lie.'

Charlotte looked at Angus. 'Shall we go and see the girl, then?'

Angus nodded. 'I'll follow you.'

Angus got out and looked towards where he had left his car. The car washers were swarming over it, and it was covered in foam. 'Great,' he whispered under his breath.

Charlotte peered out of her window. Angus indicated his car and shrugged, and she grinned.

TEN MINUTES LATER, they were on their way to see Sophie. Charlotte didn't know Taunton much at all, just that it was famous for its cider factory, racecourse and cricket ground. She wondered what other industries there were in Somerset. She'd seen plenty of farmland on the drive over. She supposed much of Taunton's business was based around that.

It didn't take them long to get to Sophie's house. It was in an affluent area, at the end of a cul-de-sac where large houses sat on large plots of land. Charlotte got out of the car just as Angus pulled up. She rang the doorbell and he arrived by her side just as the door opened.

A middle-aged woman, presumably Sophie's mother, stood there. 'Yes?'

'Mrs Lenton?' said Charlotte.

'Yes.' She looked at them both, concern on her face.

'My name is Angus Darrow, and this is Charlotte Lockwood.' He paused a moment, deciding what to say next. 'We're private investigators working for the family of a young man called Daniel Cray. He's gone missing and we are looking for him.'

She opened the door wider. 'How can I help?'

'We believe your daughter Sophie knows him, and we wanted to ask her some questions. Could we come in and talk to her? Is she in?'

She paused, taking in what they'd said. 'I suppose so.' She opened the door wider for them to enter and showed them into the front room. 'Sit down and I'll get her…' She scuttled off, leaving Angus and Charlotte alone.

Neither of them sat down, both looking around the room. It was large and high-ceilinged, with a dark leather suite. An oil painting of a red setter hung above the fireplace, while the mantlepiece held small photo frames with snapshots from holidays.

Angus picked up one photo. 'Looks like that's Sophie, and she has a younger brother.'

They heard footsteps coming downstairs. Shortly afterwards, Sophie entered the room, with her mother behind her.

She was short and slim. Her hair was shaved to the skin behind one ear, and the rest was long and dyed bright pink. She wore a gold stud in her nose and there were at least seven or eight going up the side of one ear. She was nearly wearing clothes: a mini skirt and a cropped top. Her face was heavily made-up with dark purple eye shadow and eyelash extensions. When Angus introduced himself and Charlotte, she looked bored.

They all sat down, Charlotte taking a seat next to Angus. He got out his notebook and pen. 'Thank you for agreeing to speak to us, Sophie. We're looking into the disappearance of Daniel Cray. Did you know he'd gone missing?'

'Yeah,' she replied.

'Do you know where he is?'

She shook her head.

'Was Daniel your boyfriend?' Charlotte asked.

That made her look up. 'No.' She answered as though it were an accusation, not a question.

'You've met up with him, though?'

'Yeah, but it was only a couple of times. I got the train to Exeter and we went for coffee. He was cool at first, he said he was ok about just being friends and then after the second time he messaged me and asked me out, but I said no.'

'Did he pester you about it?'

She shrugged. 'A bit, but that's not unusual. He kept asking me to meet him again, but I always said no. In the end he stopped asking.'

'And that was the end of him bothering you?'

'Yeah. Daniel's all right, you know. Harmless. Not like some boys.'

'And you're concerned about him?'

'Yeah. I mean, he wasn't the sort to go off. He liked

college, likes gaming. He was good, and the team needs him back.'

'The team? Do you mean your online team for Escape from Pirate Island?'

She nodded.

'Are you at college?' Angus asked.

While they'd been speaking, Sophie's mother had been silently watching. From her surprised expression, this was all news to her. But at the mention of college, she spoke up. 'She's taking some time off this year and exploring her options. Aren't you, dear?'

Angus and Charlotte exchanged a look.

Sophie looked at her feet. 'I started a subscriber fan page and it's doing well. I don't need to go to college.'

'Lissa!' cried Mrs Lenton. 'I told you not to mention this. Especially in front of strangers.' She looked at Charlotte and Angus, 'I don't approve. At all.'

Sophie looked up. 'I get loads of fans from TikTok. I've got nearly 300,000 followers now.' Her demeanour became more animated.

'That's a lot of followers,' Charlotte commented. 'Don't they call TikTok the internet's red light zone?'

Sophie frowned, then shrugged. 'Dunno.'

'I think it's disgusting,' Mrs Lenton piped up. 'I can't believe you're doing this, Sophie.' She turned to Angus and Charlotte. 'I've been trying to get her to stop, but she won't. She's making so much money from it now that she won't think of college or a proper job.' She addressed her daughter. 'It won't last forever. One day you'll be older and no one will want to look at you.'

'By that time I'll have made so much money. I won't need to do it anymore,' Sophie retorted. 'I want lots of money. There's nothing wrong with that,' she added, a touch defensively.

'You could be making a positive contribution to society!' Mrs Lenton snapped, and smoothed down her skirt.

Charlotte looked out of the window and spoke in a wistful tone. 'Money isn't everything, Sophie. You may think it is now, but what really matters is friends and family.'

There was a pause, then Angus's voice cut through the silence. 'Was Daniel one of your paid fans?'

'Yeah.'

'Did you ever ask him to do anything on camera?'

'No way!' She sounded utterly disgusted. 'He was a mate; I wasn't interested in him like that. Anyway, I'm the one in front of the camera, not the fans. I don't want to see what they look like or what they're doing. I just want their money.'

'So you never spoke to each other on camera? It's just that Daniel filmed himself...' Angus cleared his throat. 'He filmed himself doing a sex act and then he was black-mailed into leaving home, as well as giving them money.'

'That's nasty. It wasn't me who got him to do that.' She folded her arms and silence fell again..

Charlotte and Angus exchanged glances again. This was over and another dead end.

They took their leave and walked to their cars. 'Do you think she's telling the truth?' Charlotte asked.

'Yes, I think she is,' Angus replied. 'She's got no reason to get him into a gang because she's a woman of her own means - isn't that what they used to call women who were sex workers?'

'Looks like you were right.' Charlotte acknowledged.

Angus pushed up his glasses. 'It isn't the first time.' He smiled.

'Smugness is unbecoming, you know.'

He got into his car, still smiling, and drove off.

Chapter 19

When Angus got home, he found a text from Simon on his phone.

Got CCTV 4 night Daniel went missing. Just emailed it. Hope it's helpful. Sorry 4 delay. If u find anything connected 2 Billy's murder give me a shout. Si.

Angus switched on his computer and sure enough, there was an email from Simon with a hyperlink to the CCTV. He downloaded the files and looked through them. The CCTV covered half an hour on either side of the time when Daniel was due to meet with his blackmailer. Sure enough, at ten past six, Daniel appeared on the screen. He stopped to look in the window of a shop, then went up the passageway at the side of Boots the Chemists that led to Northernhay Gardens. He didn't reappear.

Angus took off his glasses and pinched the bridge of his nose. It had been a long shot, he'd known that, and it had missed. Whoever had met Daniel had gone to Northernhay Gardens via the back route. The route without CCTV.

~

THE NEXT MORNING, Charlotte was up early. She sent a text to Angus: *Checking out Daniel's friends Owen and Sean. Will be in touch later.*

He called her a few moments later. 'What are you doing?' he asked in an accusatory tone.

'Just tech stuff.'

'I don't like the sound of that.'

'No need to get anxious. I won't talk to them.'

'Charlotte, I appreciate your help, but I don't want you doing anything illegal.'

'You didn't mind the other day. Sorry, got to go. Speak later.' She ended the call. He called again, but she didn't pick up.

Grigore took her to Owen's house in the smaller, less conspicuous black BMW. He'd wanted to take the Bentley, but she knew it would stick out. She didn't want to attract attention; even the BMW was pushing it. She'd told Grigore not to wear his uniform either. He'd objected at first, since he loved wearing the uniform, but when she explained that it would be like having a beacon announcing their presence, he relented.

Owen lived in Alphington, a normal suburban area on the other side of the Exe. They parked a little up the road, but close enough for what Charlotte needed.

Charlotte touched the screen of her laptop and it went from blank to alive. There were over twenty Wi-Fi networks listed, but she could triangulate and pinpoint the right one. It took fifteen mins before her password cracker got in.

Just as she got access to the Wi-Fi, the front door of Owen's house opened and a teenage boy stepped out with a black Cockapoo on a lead. He sloped up the road, the eager dog practically dragging him along, and walked straight past her, his head over his smartphone. The back windows of the BMW were blacked out, anyway.

Half an hour later, she closed the laptop. 'That's it, everything is in place. I've hacked the Smart Home device and Owen's computer.'

'Vas it hard?' Grigore asked.

'Easy as pie. These foolish people using smart devices have no idea at all.'

'Iz zat him?' Grigore pointed.

Coming back down the road was Owen. He was carrying a shopping bag now, still glued to his phone.

'Yes, that's him,' said Charlotte. 'I wonder what he bought from the shop. He didn't have that bag when he left.'

'Maybe he bought it in shop.'

'It doesn't seem new. In fact, it looks as if it's been used many times. And Owen doesn't look the type to worry about recycling.'

'Suspicious, no?' Grigore stated.

'Very.'

'Where now? Home?'

'No, Sean's place.'

At four o'clock, they pulled up in front of Angus's house. 'Hello,' she said brightly as he opened the front door.

Angus was dressed in a plain white T-Shirt and dark trousers, holding a mug of tea.

He smiled when he realised it was Charlotte and looked over her shoulder.

'No Bentley today?'

'Too obvious. I have news. Can I come in?'

'Yeh, sure,' he said, and she followed him inside to the living room.

'Owen is doing something dodgy. He left his house to walk the dog and returned half an hour later with a plastic bag full of something.'

'He went shopping?' Angus raised his eyebrows. 'Very suspicious…'

Charlotte scoffed. 'No, Afterwards he sent an email: 'Package received.' If that doesn't sound dodgy, I don't know what does.'

'What do you mean, he sent an email saying 'Package received'? How did you know what he emailed?'

Charlotte's lips twisted slightly. 'You asked me not to tell you what I might or might not be doing illegally.'

Angus sighed. 'You hacked their Wi-Fi, didn't you?'

Charlotte shrugged. 'Any chance of a cup of tea?'

Angus walked to the kitchen, and she followed him. 'You realise the law applies to you too, you know?' he said as he filled the kettle. He put it down on the worktop and flicked the switch.

She stood in the kitchen doorway, watching him. 'Really? I never knew, what with being a cyber-security expert and all.'

'I don't like it.'

'No one cares if a middle-aged woman is hacking a spotty teenager on the wrong side of Exeter. Anyway, how would they find out? I'm an expert at hiding my tracks.'

There was silence until the kettle billowed steam and clicked off.

Angus poured boiling water into a cup. 'I'm sure you are. But I have a reputation to maintain.'

'Don't worry, I won't get caught. And if I do, which I won't, I'll swear you had no idea what I was doing. Girl Guide's honour.' She held up two fingers in a salute.

He looked up surprised. 'You were a Girl Guide?'

'Yep.' She paused. 'For two weeks. I hated it.'

'That's not being a Girl Guide.'

'Don't deny my lived experience. Even if it was short-lived.'

Angus sighed again and handed her a cup of tea. 'I don't see what we can do. It's not as if we can search his house, and I haven't the time to watch it. Especially as it has nothing to do with Daniel going missing.'

'But we don't know that,' said Charlotte. 'Daniel is being sextorted; what's the most likely thing he's being made to do? He's male; it's unlikely to be the sex trade. So it must be drugs. If it is drugs and his friend Owen is also trafficking or dealing, there could be a link.'

Charlotte sipped her tea and Angus took the opportunity to get a word in. 'I got the CCTV recordings for the night Daniel went missing.'

Charlotte looked at him over the rim of her cup. 'And?'

'I found Daniel but nobody else around that time.'

'Can I have a copy?'

'Sure. But I'd have thought you'd just hack into the CCTV system and take them yourself.'

She smiled. 'I probably could. But I'll stick to conventional means, seeing as you've already got access.'

'That's a relief. Look, I don't mean to be rude, but I need to get going I'm meeting workmen at my flats.'

Charlotte's brows rose up, 'You have flats?'

He nodded. 'I've been renovating them, or at least trying to. Some of the work I've done myself, but a lot of it I've had workmen in - or not in as they never seem to turn up and when they do, they bodge it up. I'm meeting a builder in an hour who I hope will actually get it done this decade.'

Charlotte assessed him for a moment, 'is that why you

left the Police? To become a property mogul? The next Donald Trump?'

He gave a short laugh. 'No. It was because of the Police taking on university graduates with absolutely no operational experience put straight in as superintendents. They've even started hiring anyone with a degree of any kind straight into being a detective. No uniform experience at all. That's what did it in the end. The stress was bad enough, but they made everything worse. One of the new recruits has a degree in Surfing - from Plymouth Uni.' Angus placed his mug down. 'They don't have a clue what they're doing. In the end, I couldn't take it anymore.'

Charlotte grimaced. 'Yes, Mark told me all about that. It's a disgrace. He hates it too. I keep telling him to leave, but for some reason he likes to inflict pain on himself.'

'He only has a few years left before he gets the full pension. Then he can be free of it.'

Charlotte didn't mention the money she'd given her brother when she'd sold the Cyber Security company. She knew he wouldn't like everyone knowing. The Police pension was a drop in the ocean compared. Her brother wanted to make a difference in the Police. It was infuriating. He could be out of it all, working for her. She wondered if he would consider working with Angus. She'd do the tech stuff, and Angus and Woody could work as a duo. No, that wouldn't do. She wanted to work with Angus alone and she liked things the way they were.

Angus looked at his watch.

'Alright, alright, I get the hint, I'll go...' Charlotte slipped off the stool. 'Hope the builder works out.' She took a last sip of tea then left.

Chapter 20

The next morning, Charlotte stood on Owen's front step and rang the doorbell. She was sure that whatever Owen was up to; it had to be connected to Daniel and she didn't care what Angus thought; she was going to find out for herself.

Grigore had dropped her off around the corner and was waiting there for her return. A man of few words, he rarely ventured an opinion about anything. But just before she had got out of the car, he had said, 'Be careful. If you no back in half hour, I come get you.'

The front door opened and a man, whom she supposed was Owen's father, stood in the doorway. Dark hair and a scruffy beard, dressed in blue jeans and an Exeter Chiefs rugby shirt. As soon as he clocked she was female, he looked her up and down. Charlotte sighed inwardly.

He leaned casually against the door frame. 'Yeah?'

'Hello,' she said cheerfully in a strong Essex accent. 'My name is Mandy Smith, and I'm from South West Electrical.'

He stared at her. 'Yeah?'

'Head Office has sent me. I understand you've been having problems with getting a smart meter fitted?'

'Yeah, but it's sorted now.' He unpeeled himself from the door frame and started to close the door. Charlotte put her hand on the door. 'South West Electrical are very sorry that you received a less than perfect service, and we'd like to help remedy that situation by offering you LED light bulbs throughout the house, free of charge. And £100 in cash.' She held up five twenty-pound notes, then consulted her clipboard. 'Can I come in? Then I can give you your money.' Always appeal to their greed.

He stared at the cash, 'Yeah, OK,' and stepped aside.

Ridiculously easy, she thought. She'd primed the clipboard with a few sheets of letterhead paper that she'd faked earlier, and around her neck was a lanyard with a fake photo ID she'd made at the same time. She'd hacked into his email —such a stupidly easy password—and his emails had revealed the whole sorry story of the smart meter. They'd been let down twice after taking the day off work, and he'd sent the electric company a stern email.

Charlotte turned and grasped the handle of her wheelie case. Inside was a variety of LED bulbs which she'd got Helena to purchase for her. She hefted it over the threshold. 'Thank you.'

He showed her through to the living room and she sat down. He followed her lead and sat opposite.

'We take complaints very seriously at South West Electrical and therefore we would like to offer you £100 in cash and free LED light bulbs, which are an energy-efficient way to reduce your electricity bills. They use 75% less electricity than ordinary bulbs and last 25% longer. If you just sign here...'

She handed him the clipboard, and he signed it. He kept his eyes on the cash.

'Great, I'll start upstairs. I'll give you the cash when I've finished.' She stood up.

'Er, OK.'

Charlotte shimmied out of the room and carried the bag upstairs. He followed her; she had rather hoped he wouldn't. She opened her case and took out a foldable stepladder, unfolded it and started with the landing light. As she reached up to the bulb, she glanced at him in the long mirror on the landing and spotted him behind her, staring at her legs. The short skirt had worked. She coughed as a small cloud of dust fell from the lampshade.

Then she moved onto the nearest room, clearly Owen's from the pungent smell of teenage boy drifting from the room. She went in. He wasn't there and for a moment, she panicked. Had he already taken the bag?

'Sorry about the mess,' said Owen's dad. He'd seen her glancing around the room and assumed the disgusting teenage mess of crisp packets, clothes and empty bottles was the problem, but Charlotte was looking for the plastic bag. There it was, tucked under the computer desk.

She turned to him. 'It's all right; I have two boys myself, and they're just as bad. Kids, eh?' She giggled and fluttered her eyelashes. 'Can I ask you a favour? I'm absolutely gasping for a drink of water. Would you mind?'

'All right.' He turned and walked downstairs, and as soon as he was out of earshot, she grabbed the bag and peered inside. It was crammed with what looked like hundreds of small bags of white pills.

'I knew it,' she muttered. Owen was trafficking drugs.

She grabbed one of the pill bags and put it in her pocket, then scanned the room. Nothing seemed unusual. She'd hacked his computer, of course, so there was no need to check that. She checked inside the wardrobe; the clothes were surprisingly neat and tidy. All designer gear, and an extensive collection of trainers. The shelves were piled with comics, but no college books were visible.

Charlotte opened a drawer: more clothes. She had a feel under the chest, but found nothing. What about under the bed? That was always where she'd hidden things: in her case as a teenager, her stash of Mills and Boon romance novels. No one had ever found them, not to her knowledge anyway. She knelt down and peered.

'What are you doing?' said a gruff voice.

Bang. Charlotte bumped her head on the bed. She'd been too busy checking the room to hear Owen's father coming back upstairs.

'Ouch, sorry, I dropped the lightbulb and it rolled under the bed.' She held up the bulb she had in her hand and the other one went to the back of her head where she'd banged it. 'I'm such a butterfingers sometimes.' She stood up and fluttered her eyelashes at him again. 'Is that my water? Thank you sooooo much.' She took the glass from him and sipped some water, then gave it back to him, climbed the ladder and started changing the bulb.

'Isn't it terrible about that missing boy?' she said, conversationally. 'David, I think it is. There are posters everywhere.'

'Daniel. Yeah, bad news. My son knows him, you know.' It sounded like a brag.

'Really?' she said in an overly awed tone.

'Yeah, they go to college together.'

'How awful. Are they close?'

'I don't know; he doesn't say, really. You know what teenage boys are like. They don't tell you much.'

Clearly. She doubted very much that Owen had confided to his father that he was shifting drugs. Ten minutes later, she'd changed all the bulbs in the house and handed the money over.

She paused at the front door. 'Well, that's it from me. Thank you for being so understanding. We hope we won't lose your custom?'

'Oh, no,' he said. 'Certainly not. Thanks so much.'

'Oh good.' She flashed a beaming smile at him, then made a point of looking him up and down. 'Well, bye then.'

She sashayed down the street until she got round the corner. Grigore was waiting in the car. He saw her and got out to open the door. 'You go home?' he asked.

'No. I need to see Angus first.'

As soon as she got in the car, she rang him, and after a few rings, it went to voicemail.

When she pulled up at Angus's house, his car was there, but after knocking, then banging on the door, she gave up. 'Damn you, Angus Darrow, where are you?' she shouted.

'What have I done?'

She whirled around. 'Angus!' She looked him up and down. He was dressed in running gear, rather sweaty, and a little short of breath. 'There you are. I've been trying to get hold of you.'

'I went for a run. I don't take my phone with me.'

'Really?'

'I try not to use it as much as possible.'

'How do you know how far you've run?' Charlotte's tone was an accusation spoken to his tight running shorts. Then she realised where she'd been looking, and her gaze shot up to his face. She felt herself flush.

'GPS watch.' He held up his wrist and smiled.

'Wait, I didn't think you were keen on tech?'

'It was a birthday gift from my daughter. She set it up for me and showed me how to work it.'

Charlotte nodded. 'What happens if you get into trouble? The watch won't help.'

'What sort of trouble would I get into?' A soft curve of a smile appeared on his lips.

Charlotte shrugged. 'Twist your ankle? Get robbed?'

'I'm less likely to get robbed with no phone.'

He had a point.

Angus pulled out a key from a small pocket in his shorts and opened the front door. Charlotte followed him into the house. 'I got into Owen's house and found the bag. It's definitely drugs – look!' She held up the little bag she'd stolen.

Angus took it from her and examined it. 'Probably prescription painkillers that are being resold. How many were there?'

'A carrier bag full. I reckon at least three hundred. If he's delivering drugs, he might be involved with Daniel going missing, it's worth looking into.'

He nodded. 'You might be right. We need to get Owen followed as soon as possible. I'll get changed and then I'll go and watch him.' He walked to the kitchen door.

'No need. I've put a GPS tag in the bag so I'll get a text message when it moves.'

Angus frowned. 'A GPS tag? Won't he find it? How big is it?'

'He won't spot it.'

'OK.' He exhaled. 'So Owen's delivering drugs. Who for? And are they the same people who are blackmailing Daniel?'

Charlotte's phone pinged and she glanced at it. 'The drugs are on the move.'

Chapter 21

They spotted him walking up Sidwell Street, in the top part of the main shopping area. It was where the independent shops were located: barbers, charity shops, health food, and takeaways. Owen looked smarter than he had before and held the carrier bag as though it were his shopping. Angus drove past him and pulled into a parking bay on the same side of the street. Owen walked past them, then into a charity shop for a local charity.

Ten minutes later, he still hadn't come out.

'What's he doing in there?' Charlotte checked her phone. The app indicated the drugs hadn't moved.

'He might be waiting for the person who's picking the bag up.'

'I'll go in and see,' Charlotte said. 'You stay here: he's met you.'

Angus unbuckled his seatbelt. 'That doesn't matter; I'm not letting you go in there alone.'

Charlotte stared at him for a moment, then relented. There was nothing she could say to stop him. She put her phone into her coat pocket, and they went into the shop together.

The charity shop was crammed with items: mostly clothes, bags and shoes. At the back was a large bookshelf. A few people were browsing, taking their time. Owen was nowhere to be seen.

Angus walked to the back of the shop, where there was a door leading to the sorting area. Charlotte watched him move closer to it, then open it and slip through.

Angus moved carefully past the bags of unsorted donations towards a further room. Then he saw that the emergency exit door was open. Owen stood in the doorway talking to a boy in a hoody who looked no more than fifteen, and who now held the plastic bag. Suddenly, Owen turned his head and looked straight at Angus, and his eyes widened in recognition. He muttered something to the boy, who ran, and slammed the door shut before Angus could reach it.

'You're in trouble, young man,' Angus shouted. He pushed the door open and looked out, but the boy was long gone.

He went back into the shop pretending to browse the book shelf. 'Track the bag; it's been handed over.'

Charlotte pulled out her phone, and they watched the GPS tracker moving down side streets. They got back into the car, and Charlotte directed him as it moved.

'Straight on,' she stated. The app showed both the tracker and them in the car as dots on the map.

'It looks like he's moving out towards Heavitree...' she commented a moment later, 'drive slower, or we'll pass him.'

'I'm only doing 15 miles an hour and I've got someone up my arse.' Angus looked in the rear-view mirror. The other driver was flashing their lights to get past. He pulled over to allow them to pass and they beeped their horn loudly as they zoomed away.

'What a tosser,' Charlotte stated. Then looked at her phone again. 'He's gone next left, quick, quick- ' she shouted.

Angus glanced at her. 'Do you shout at Grigore when he's driving you?'

They turned left. The road was a cul-de-sac with rows of Victorian terraced houses.

Charlotte stared at her phone. 'It's stopped.'

She directed him, driving slower now until they reached the end of the road. Angus parked, and they got out of the car. The street was empty.

Charlotte followed the signal, then bent down and picked up what looked like a pen. 'They found it.'

They stared at each other for a moment. 'Damn it,' Charlotte said. 'How did they know?'

'Maybe they worked it out,' said Angus.

Charlotte sighed. 'It's pretty indistinguishable from other pens for a reason. I need a micro tracker next time.'

Angus raised his eyebrows. 'Next time?'

Charlotte shrugged. 'I'm going back to the charity shop to speak to Owen.'

'I'll come with you.'

But back at the shop, Owen was nowhere to be seen.

Angus approached the elderly lady behind the till. 'Is Owen around?'

'No, dear, he ran off about five minutes ago saying he was unwell. Mr McInlay won't be happy; he's supposed to be here for at least two hours every week.'

'Mr McInlay? From City College?'

'That's right, dear, he sends all sorts of youngsters here. Some are nice, like that young lad Daniel who's gone missing. Others, not so much.'

'Daniel worked here?'

'Yes, dear.'

'How long had he been with you before he went missing?'

She thought for a moment. 'Not long, maybe a few weeks. I showed him the ropes, such a polite young man. I had no idea he would run off like that. Such a shame. I hope he comes back; his parents must be beside themselves.'

'He didn't mention running away?' Angus asked.

'Not to me. He seemed happy enough. He wasn't used to work–I had to show him how to do even the simplest things–but he never complained and he was always polite. Not like some of them. Right cheeky buggers, a few of them, including that Owen. I won't be sorry to see the back of him.'

'How long do they spend volunteering here?'

'A couple of months, just for a few hours a week. Mr McInlay says it helps them to build character and develops community spirit. Most of them haven't a clue what to do, though. Of course, we don't let them near the money; they just sort through the donations.'

'Thanks.'

They left the shop and stopped outside. 'So the college tutor is sending students to a charity shop that is being used to traffic drugs under the volunteers' noses,' said Charlotte. 'Coincidence?'

'I need to speak to McInlay,' Angus replied in a serious tone.

'And one of the boys was Daniel.' Charlotte reminded him.

If he had still been in the police, he might have had Mr McInlay questioned and followed. But he wasn't any more; he was just one man. Yet it was rather suspicious that

Daniel had been volunteering at the charity shop and Owen had been distributing drugs from there too.'I'll do another search on Owen's computer.'

Angus frowned. 'Have you accessed his computer before?'

Charlotte avoided eye contact. 'No, absolutely not. That would be illegal.'

He raised an eyebrow. 'I don't believe you.'

'Good. I'm not accessing his computer and I haven't done it before,' Charlotte said, deadpan.

'I'm going to see Owen. You stay out of trouble.'

Chapter 22

Angus knocked on Owen's front door and, after a few moments, he opened it. When he saw Angus he tried to close it again, but Angus's foot was in the way.

'Owen, I need to talk to you about earlier.'

'There's nothing to talk about.'

'You know there is. If you're being blackmailed into delivering drugs, I can help.'

'Keep your voice down,' he muttered.

'Let me in and we can talk. Quietly.'

After a few moments, Owen opened the door and Angus stepped inside. 'Are your parents in?'

'Dad's out back, doing something in the shed.'

'I'm guessing you don't want him to know you've been trafficking drugs.'

'Dunno know what you're talking about,' his voice was deadpan, but his eyes were wide.

'Don't be smart with me, son. You're shifting pills.'

Owen's mouth fell open. Angus had honed his skill in sounding intimidating in the police, and he hadn't lost it.

'I want to know where Daniel is.'

'I told you, I don't know.'

'Don't lie to me. Who are you working for?'

'Yeah, I really want to commit suicide by telling you,' he spat.

'Are you working for the people who've got Daniel?'

'I told you, I don't know about Daniel. They give me instructions and that's it. I'm on the bottom rung; I just deliver stuff and don't ask questions.'

Angus was pretty good at telling when someone was lying. He didn't think Owen was.

'You'd better not be lying. If you are, I'll make sure your gang leaders think you've been talking.'

Owen walked into the living room and sat on the settee, his head in his hands. 'You can't tell anyone. I've tried to stop, but they won't let me.'

'I know some people in the police who can help you.'

'I don't want help from the police. You've got no evidence, anyway. It's your word against mine.'

'Yes, but my word means much more than yours.'

Owen looked up at him. 'Do what you like; I'll never admit anything.'

Angus left. In the car, he phoned Simon and told him about Owen. Boys like him were used by gang members; the police were interested in the organ grinders, not the monkeys. He needed to talk to McInlay again and find out exactly what was going on.

~

ANGUS ENTERED the Computing building again. McInlay wasn't in his office, so he walked down the corridor looking for him. Each room had row upon row of computers. Some were full of students, others were empty.

When Angus returned to the office, McInlay was sitting at his desk. 'Can I have another word?' he asked.

McInlay was typing away, head down. 'Sorry, I just need to finish this email.'

Angus sat down in the chair opposite, waiting for him to finish. He'd rarely had to wait for anyone when he'd been in the police; the title of Detective Inspector had ensured respect from people like McInlay.

Eventually McInlay stopped typing, clicked his mouse and looked up. 'Sorry about that, I had to get an email to a parent before five. Have you found Daniel?'

'Not yet.'

'That's a shame. What can I help you with?'

'You send some of your students to volunteer at a charity shop in Exeter.'

McInlay took off his glasses. 'Yes, that's right. My mother volunteers there, so I send her the kids who need some work experience for their CV.'

'How long have you been sending them there?'

He thought for a moment. 'A few years. At least two, it might even be three. Why?'

'Did you send Owen there?'

'Hmm, let me see.' He put his glasses back on, looked at the computer and clicked his mouse. 'Yes, I sent Owen. He's about to finish his three-month stint.'

'Did you know he was using the shop to distribute drugs?'

McInlay blinked at him. 'Drugs?' He laughed nervously. 'You're serious?'

'I am. He's been passing drugs through the shop. I don't know how long for, but I'm guessing it's the entire time he's worked there.'

McInlay frowned, then sat back in his chair. 'What evidence do you have for this?'

'I followed him and I have obtained a sample of the goods, which I've just passed on to Devon and Cornwall Police.'

McInlay flushed, tensed, and been unable to answer him at first, then he spoke. 'The little swine. I gave him this opportunity, and he threw it back in my face. Wait - you don't think I'm involved?'

'Are you?'

'No! I despise drugs. I didn't even experiment in my youth.' He straightened his back and lifted his chin in defence of his words.

'So you know nothing about it.'

'Of course I don't. I've seen too many students fall into drug addiction and ruin their lives.'

Angus assessed McInlay's response; over the years, he'd got good at it. He had looked guilty, but ironically, that made Angus sure he was telling the truth. Guilty people were usually cool and calm, because they were prepared. And either way, the police would arrive soon to question McInlay formally.

'I suggest you get the staff in the shop to monitor the students more closely, Mr McInlay.' Angus knew it sounded patronising, but he didn't care. 'By the way, why didn't you tell me that Daniel was volunteering there?'

McInlay stared at him. 'I thought I had.'

'No, you didn't.'

'It must have slipped my mind. I have a lot of responsibilities, and sometimes I forget things.' He shifted under Angus's gaze. 'Is that all?'

Angus got up. 'For now.'

Chapter 23

As he drove home, Angus thought that if McInlay was involved in drugs, he was sure the truth would out. There was nothing he despised more than adults who took advantage of children or young adults, and it would mean a scourge on the reputation of the college. He'd seen too many lives destroyed by drugs over the years.

Not long after he was back at home, his phone rang. It was Charlotte.

'Did you find anything out from Owen or Mr McInlay?' She asked the moment he'd answered.

'Hello Charlotte. I'm fine thanks, how are you?'

'Er, sorry. Well, did you?'

Angus rubbed his forehead. 'No. Owen wouldn't talk and McInlay denied knowing anything about the drug dealing at the shop.'

'Do you believe him?'

'I think so. He seemed genuinely shocked. I've told the police and they can deal with it now. If they find out anything useful about Daniel, they'll let us know.'

There was silence for a few moments, then Charlotte's

tone softened. 'Why don't you come over for dinner? Don't worry, I won't make a pass at you again. Helena and Grigore are here too.'

He wasn't expecting that. Part of him was curious to see what sort of relationship Charlotte, Helena and Grigore had. And despite her unpredictability, she was starting to grow on him. She was smart and attractive, there wasn't much not to like. She was also loaded, and no doubt had men lined up to get close to her. 'When do you want me?' He found himself saying.

'Whenever you're ready.'

Half an hour later, Angus rang Charlotte's doorbell and Helena answered.

Her frown turned to a broad smile. 'Mr Angus! Come, come.' She beckoned him in. 'I so pleased you come. You good man. You turn down Charlotte when she throw herself on you.'

Angus stepped inside, momentarily speechless.

He had refused her, but a tiny part of him knew that if she'd been sober, he might not have turned her down. He pushed that thought aside. This was a professional relationship, and it was better for everyone if it stayed that way.

'Hello,' Charlotte called from the dining-room door. 'Come and take a seat.'

He walked through. She stood on the other side of a large solid oak table big enough to sit at least twelve people. She was wearing a dress again, but this time it was long with short sleeves, a v-neck with blue and red kaleidoscope patterns. On the table was a plate of pickled vegetables and lots of homemade bread. 'What can I get you to drink?' She asked.

'Just some water, please.' He stood in front of a chair and she beckoned him to sit. She disappeared into the kitchen and returned with a bottle of mineral water. That hadn't been what he meant; tap water would have been fine. He wondered if all multi-millionaires avoided tap water. The aroma of whatever Helena was cooking wafted through and Angus's stomach rumbled. He hadn't realised how hungry he was.

He heard the front door open and a moment later, Grigore came in and sat next to Angus. He nodded at him, then took out his smartphone and stared at it.

Charlotte gave Grigore a glass too and set the table.

Helena came through with the food. 'Here we are,' she said, setting down a large dish filled with cylindrical minced meat rolls.

'It's called Mici,' Charlotte said to Angus. 'My favourite Romanian dish. It's minced beef and pork.'

'And my special secret spices. I tell no one,' Helena added.

'Not even me,' Grigore said, helping himself.

'Or me,' said Charlotte. 'Is there anyone you'd give your recipe to, Helena?'

Helena rolled her eyes. 'If I tell secret recipe, it not secret!'

Conversation ceased for a few minutes as they ate.

'So how did you and Charlotte meet, Helena?' Angus asked. He was curious. He'd worked out there was some kind of bond between them, but wasn't sure what it was.

'Ah, now, I work for Charlotte as cleaner at Cyber Security company.' Helena sipped her water and put her knife and fork down.

'How did a cleaner get to know the owner of such a large company?'

'She work late, I work late. We start talk in kitchen. She lovely and not care me just cleaner.'

Angus took another bite of the mici. It had just the right balance of spices. He liked it.

'We used to have such lovely chats, didn't we?' Charlotte gushed, 'but that wasn't just it though, was it? Can I tell him?' Charlotte asked Helena.

Helena nodded.

'I noticed after about six months that Helena had bruises on her arms. Then one evening, she had a black eye. So I offered to get her into a refuge there and then.'

Helena continued, 'She drive me herself, I leave nasty man. She come every day to make sure I OK. Then offer me job to work with her, not just cleaner.'

'And what happened to your partner?' Angus asked. 'Was he prosecuted?' They hadn't mentioned the partner, but Angus had come across enough cases of domestic violence to know that's who it would have been.

'That when I come over from Romania, Helena my cousin,' said Grigore. 'I sort him out.' He didn't even look up from his plate as he stuffed food in his mouth.

The result took little guesswork. Grigore, although short, was a stocky, intimidating man. Perhaps that was better justice.

'Grigore was thinking about coming over here anyway, and he's stayed too. And here we all are!' Charlotte finished.

'I like caring for Charlotte,' said Helena. 'Much better than cleaning, but she need help after bastard husband leave with best friend.' Helena winked her nose. 'She stupid bitch,' she spat. 'She always want everything Charlotte have.'

Angus stole a glance at Charlotte. She had stopped eating and was staring out of the window.

Helena didn't seem to notice. 'Charlotte, she cry for weeks. I here to comfort her and pay back what she did for me.'

'Her brother sort him out, though,' Grigore said, then laughed a deep, long laugh that made his shoulders shake.

'Shh!' Helena glared at Grigore.

'Is that the favour you owe him?' Angus asked, spearing a mici.

Charlotte's mouth turned up at the corner. 'I can neither confirm nor deny that,' she said eventually, with a sly glance.

That was a yes, then. He wondered what Woody had done to Charlotte's ex. It must have been big. Woody had said she owed him a lot, and he knew Woody could get ... passionate about things.

'You're wondering why I owe him so much,' Charlotte commented.

'I am.'

'I won't tell. He might.' She paused. 'So, Angus is a Scottish name, but your accent is English. What's that all about then?'

Angus sipped his water and put down the glass. 'Good deflection Charlotte. My parents are both Scottish; they moved to Devon when I was five.'

'That explains the name Angus then, and the lack of a Scottish accent. Where did they move to?'

'Devonport. Dad worked in the shipyards as an electrician.'

'Do they still live here?'

'No, they moved back when they retired. They're in Stirling now.'

He'd often been asked about his name; at school, they had teased him about it. Devon boys weren't called Angus. They were called Phillip, David, Michael or Peter. Then, when any of his friends met his parents, they laughed about their accents.

'Your life would be very different if they'd stayed in

Scotland.' Charlotte took hold of her glass and turned it a little.

'It would. My family in Glasgow all wanted me to live and work up there, but I've always been happy in Devon.'

'Devon very beautiful. But ruined by tourists. Annoying bastards.' Grigore said between mouthfuls of food.

'I can't deny it,' said Angus with a small laugh. 'The grockles are a necessary evil, though. We need their money, but they're irritating as hell.'

Helena frowned. 'What is this grockle?'

Angus lifted the bottle and poured some more water into his glass. 'The Devon term for tourists. Don't tell anyone, especially the tourists themselves.' He smiled, then his phone rang, and he looked at the display. 'It's Daniel's mother. I'd better take it.'

He stood up and went into the lounge. Charlotte, Helena and Grigore sat silent, desperately trying to hear Angus's end of the call.

A few minutes later, he came back in and sat down. 'Unfortunately, Mr and Mrs Cray have almost run out of money, so we'll have to stop the investigation soon. They'd applied for a loan from the bank, but were refused.'

'What about the crowd funder?' Charlotte asked.

'It's only raised about five hundred pounds and they won't get that for another couple of weeks.'

'How long have we got to find Daniel before the money runs out?'

'Two days,' Angus stated.

Charlotte spoke in a confident voice, 'well then, we'll just have to find him before then.'

Chapter 24

Charlotte arrived at Angus's house at ten-thirty the next morning with coffee, a box of pastries, and an A1 cardboard envelope. She went through to the kitchen and he followed her. Wearing a pair of dark blue skinny jeans, white top and denim jacket, Angus thought she looked the antithesis of the woman he'd first met that first morning a few days ago, and when she'd looked like she'd been dragged through a hedge. Several times.

'You been for another run?' She opened the pastry box and sat down on one of the breakfast bar chairs. 'Go on, have one.'

'Very observant. You should join the police.' He was still in his running gear and was about to refuse, but they smelt freshly baked and he had run ten kilometers. He took a cinnamon swirl.

'So what next, Angus Darrow?' She took a bite of a pastry and watched him eat his. 'Ooo, I nearly forgot–I was busy last night.' She stood up, opened the huge cardboard envelope and pulled out a cork board covered with photos, printed words and strings kept in by drawing pins.

'I've done a conspiracy board. I thought it might help us to focus.'

Angus almost choked on his pastry, but Charlotte didn't notice. She held up the board, smiling at him. 'I've put all the prime suspects on it. The College Tutor, David the Computer Tutor from the Cafe, The Scout Master Kenneth, Sean, Owen. I've put Isabelle on too. Even though she's a red herring and seemingly not connected, I thought I should include her for completeness. What do you think?' She looked at him like a child showing a parent her artwork.

Angus stared at the board, then at Charlotte. He put his hand over his eyes. 'Charlotte.'

'What is it? Have I forgotten something?'

'No, I don't think so. It's very ... thorough.'

'Oh good!' She beamed at him. 'I spent ages searching online for the best way to do it. I even went on the Deep Web. Loads of people there are looking into conspiracies and cold case murders. There's a whole industry based around solving crimes. There are even chat rooms where amateur sleuths work together.' She shot him a speculative glance.

'It's just...'

She raised her eyebrows. 'What?'

'Nothing. It's a work of art.' He took another bite of his pastry, then placed it on the counter. 'I'm going to have a shower.'

Charlotte went into the dining room, propped the board up on the table and contemplated it.

'Who is behind this?' She studied the photo of Daniel Cray in the middle of the board. 'It has to be someone you know.'

As she studied the board, the doorbell rang. 'I'll get it,' she shouted, up the stairs and answered the door.

A short, dark-haired woman stood on the doorstep. She looked Charlotte up and down. 'Who are you?' she asked, raising an eyebrow.

'Who are *you*?' Charlotte replied, her heckles up.

'I'm Angus's ex-wife. Is he in?' She looked past Charlotte.

'Yes.' Charlotte didn't move.

Rhona sighed. 'Can I come in?'

Charlotte shrugged and walked into the house, leaving the door open, and Rhona followed her through to the kitchen.

'Tea? Coffee?' Charlotte asked.

'No, thanks,' Rhona snapped. 'Where is he?'

'He's in the shower,' Charlotte said with a meaningful smile. 'I'm sure he'll be down soon.' She sipped her coffee and watched Rhona over the rim of the cup.

Rhona caught sight of the pastries on the table. 'Would you like one?' She asked in a sickly sweet tone.

'No, thanks.'

They stared at each other, sizing each other up.

'I'll wait. I need to speak to him.' Rhona leaned against the counter and folded her arms. Eventually, Angus came downstairs dressed in his usual smart trousers and a white shirt and appeared at the kitchen door. He stopped dead as soon as he saw his ex-wife. 'Rhona,' he said, quickly.

'Angus,' she replied, equally briskly.

'What do you want?'

'Well, that's charming. I need to speak to you and you aren't answering my calls.'

'I've been busy.'

'So I see,' she said, giving Charlotte a long look.

Charlotte raised her eyebrows. 'Don't mind me, I'm not listening.' She took another sip of her coffee.

'Charlotte, would you mind leaving us to talk?' Angus asked.

She smiled. 'Anything you say, Angus,' she said demurely. She gave Rhona a sidelong glance as she left the room.

Angus sat down on the nearest stool. 'What is it?'

'I'm trying to arrange Grace's twenty-first party.'

'I hadn't forgotten. It's in a few days.'

'I need the money for the room hire and the caterers, as we agreed.'

'How much?'

'Four hundred.'

Angus shifted on the stool. 'What are you serving, caviar?'

'No. Everything's expensive these days.'

'Is that half the cost?'

'Yes, I'm paying the same.'

'OK, I'll transfer the money later.'

'Thank you.'

Rhona leaned against the kitchen cupboard. 'So who's the blonde? I didn't realise you were putting it out there.'

'Just a colleague. She's helping with my current case.'

Rhona raised her eyebrows.

He could insist, but part of him wanted to make her jealous. 'She's very good at her job.'

'I'm sure she is.' the corner of her mouth turned into a smile.

'It's none of your business, anyway.'

Rhona stood up straight. 'You're right. We're adults, and what you do or don't do with her is your business.'

'How is Brian, anyway?'

'It's Malcolm, as you well know. He's fine, thank you.'

'Has he proposed yet?'

'No, and I don't want him to. We're happy as we are.'

She glared at him, and he didn't bother answering her. 'I'll keep you updated with the party.' She walked towards the door., 'You're invited, by the way.'

He watched her leave the kitchen.

Charlotte looked up from her laptop as Rhona walked past. 'Bye,' she said.

Rhona lifted her chin and left the house.

Angus came into the living room a few moments later.

'She's charm personified,' Charlotte commented.

'She thought we were an item and she seemed strangely annoyed. What are you doing?' Angus asked.

'Still checking through the CCTV?'

'Any luck?'

'I'm not sure. Look at this.' Charlotte turned the laptop round and pressed play. The recording was from one camera on the lower part of Exeter's High Street. 'Here.' She paused the video, then pointed to two figures. 'Isn't that Daniel's aunt, Janet?'

'It is.' Angus looked more closely.

'Who's the man she's with? Is that her husband, Billy? He's a bit old for her.'

Angus stared at the screen. 'That isn't her husband. That's Kenneth Webster, Daniel's Scout leader.'

Chapter 25

Angus rang Kenneth Webster's doorbell and glanced at Charlotte. 'Let me do the talking, all right?'

She smiled at him. 'Yes, boss.'

Kenneth's car was on the drive, and another was parked there too: a small red Ford.

Kenneth answered the door. His gaze shifted between Charlotte and Angus.

'Mr Webster, would you mind if we had a quick word?' Angus spoke in a polite tone, not giving away why they were there.

'Er, no. Hold on a minute.' Kenneth closed the door, and they could see he moved away. They looked at each other. 'What's he up to?' Charlotte asked. Then, a short time later, the door opened, and he showed them in.

Angus sat in the same seat as last time, with Charlotte next to him and Kenneth opposite. 'This is Charlotte Lockwood,' he said. 'She's helping me find Daniel.'

'And how can I help?' asked Kenneth, looking at Angus. 'How is it going?'

'Mr Webster, I'm here to ask how you know Daniel's aunt, Janet.'

'Janet?' He flicked a glance at the door. He was a terrible liar.

'I see you know each other,' Angus replied.

'Oh yes, Janet! Silly me. I only know her because sometimes she dropped Daniel off at Scouts.'

'So what were you doing near Northernhay Gardens with her on the day Daniel went missing?'

'Erm…' He paused, his brow furrowed. 'We just ran into one another in the park and we had a chat.'

'That's it?'

'That's it.'

'So what is her car doing on your drive?'

Kenneth's gaze moved to the window this time. 'Car?'

'The red Ford outside. I saw it last week when I met her at Daniel's house. Don't try to deny it.'

They heard footsteps, and Janet appeared in the doorway. 'It's all right, Kenneth.' She came in the room and stood beside his chair. 'We're seeing each other.'

'How long has that been going on for?' asked Angus.

'About a year, but we need it kept quiet. Our relationship has nothing to do with Daniel going missing. Billy and me still lived together, but we drifted apart years ago. Not sure why we bothered keeping up the pretence.'

'Did Billy know you were seeing each other?'

'No.'

'What about your sister?'

'She doesn't know either. I will tell her. I'm going to be moving in with Kenneth soon. With Billy gone so soon, I couldn't do it just yet. Especially with Daniel missing.'

'What were you both doing in Exeter on the evening that Daniel went missing?' Angus asked.

'We met up in a cafe. We couldn't meet at my house,

obviously, and we enjoy going out and having coffee together. It's like being teenagers again.'

'Did you see Daniel on the night he went missing?'

'No, I'd have remembered. He's my nephew.'

Something definitely didn't feel right, and it wasn't the age gap. Kenneth must be at least twenty-five years older than Janet. But Angus said nothing. From the state of her house, Janet wasn't well off, and by her own admission Billy had a gambling problem. Perhaps she was using Kenneth to secure her future.

'I may have cheated on Billy,' she continued, 'but our marriage broke down years ago. We just stayed together because it was easier.'

Kenneth looked Angus in the eyes. 'I know you think I'm too old for her, but what we've got, it's love. When you get to my age, you realise you've little time left and you live life to the full.'

Janet smiled down at him. 'Age is just a number,' she said. 'We're all young at heart.' Then she looked at Angus. 'Did you hear the good news? An anonymous person left a massive donation on Daniel's crowd funder. Thousands, apparently. Can you believe it? Now Mary and Douglas can afford to hire you for a lot longer.'

'Oh, really?' Angus raised his eyebrows at Charlotte, who gave him an innocent look.

～

OUTSIDE, Angus stopped Charlotte. 'You gave the money to the Crays, didn't you?'

'I have no idea what you are talking about,' she said nonchalantly.

He sighed. 'You're a terrible liar, Charlotte.'

'Why would you think it was me?' she said, attempting to look innocent.

'It's no coincidence that the Crays get a huge anonymous donation the day after they told me they'd run out of money, is it? And you're one of very few people who know that.'

'What makes you think I donated ten thousand—'

'I'm not stupid, Charlotte. Who else would it be? And by the way, Janet didn't tell us how much was donated.'

Charlotte made a face. 'All right, it was me.'

Angus gave her a serious look. 'Why did you do that?'

'Why? Why do you think?'

'For goodness sake, Charlotte, stop interfering. If they run out of money, that's their problem.'

She walked up to him, grabbed his jacket lapels, and looked him in the eyes. 'Look, I need this investigation. This is the first time since Idris left me that I actually want to get out of bed in the morning. I have a purpose. I have something to take my mind off the fact I can't work in my own field for the next three years and that my husband left me for my best friend. My mental health is a hundred times better, and my therapist says I need to keep doing this. I *need* this.'

Angus stared back at her, and for a moment, they were standing, looking into each other's eyes. Then he gently worked her fingers free from his jacket.

She continued, 'They opened a crowd funder and I donated. What's wrong with that?' Her tone was calmer. 'It's my money and I can do what I like with it. And if I'd given you the money directly, there's no way you'd have accepted it.'

Angus took a step back, still looking at her. He flexed his neck and straightened his collar and tie.

'See,' said Charlotte.

'I need to stand on my own two feet. I can't have you giving me money.'

'I didn't give you the money. I gave it to the Crays' crowd funder to find their son. They hired you.'

'It comes down to the same thing. I need to do this on my own.'

'Did you do everything in the police on your own, or was it a team effort?'

He stared at her for a moment. She was insufferably right too much of the time. 'That isn't the point.'

'Yes, it is. Stop being so proud. I won't tell anyone that I gave the donation. I already have enough people begging me for money; I can't be doing with any more. Anyway, why does it matter where the Crays' money came from? The point is that you can continue finding Daniel and I can help.'

He stepped back again, leaning against the car.

'I bet you didn't join the police for the money. I reckon you wanted to make a difference. This is making a difference.'

He took a deep breath. Charlotte seemed to push the wrong and the right buttons at the same time.

She frowned. 'I just want to find Daniel and help with my mental health. Kill two birds with one stone, if you like.' She took a step towards him and placed her hands flat on his lapels this time. 'Look at it this way: I'm buying my own recovery. It has nothing to do with you. It's all about me and Daniel.'

He raised an eyebrow. Despite pushing his buttons, she also had the ability to win him over.

'I know that sounds completely narcissistic and selfish, but doing this with you has really helped me. And I do genuinely want to find Daniel. I have two sons of my own and I don't know what I would do if this happened to either of them. I'd go stark raving mad.'

She dropped her hands away, and Angus covered his face with his hands. 'Aargh.' When he emerged, he still looked tense. 'All right, Charlotte, we'll carry on, but I'm still annoyed with you.'

Charlotte grinned. 'I don't care. This is about me and Daniel, remember?'

'You've got to promise me you won't do this again.'

'No.' She folded her arms. 'You don't get to tell me what to do with my money. Nobody does.'

'You're bloody insufferable.' He shook his head, but there was a glimmer of a smile on his face.

'I know. But I don't care.'

Chapter 26

Angus went home and spent the rest of the day thinking about possible avenues of investigation. He even studied Charlotte's conspiracy board in case it helped. He remembered her eager face when she had pulled it out of the huge envelope. She was exasperating. But also clever, attractive and thoroughly annoying. Ten thousand pounds she'd donated to the crowd funder. He supposed that was small change to her. He wondered what she was doing. Probably hacking someone else's computer. It was all rather depressing.

There hadn't been a single indication of where Daniel might be. Earlier, he had phoned Simon to see if there was any more information about Billy's murder, but they were still waiting for the forensic evidence to be processed. Despite being funded to find Daniel, he'd hit a brick wall.

At six o'clock, he heard a knock at the door. He knew who it was, but wasn't sure he wanted to see her right now. He should have gone to the cinema, or the indoor climbing wall. Somewhere out for a change.

He sat, waiting, and a few moments later, the doorbell

rang. 'Angus, let me in!' Charlotte shouted through the letterbox. 'I'm not going away. Open the door!'

He sighed, got up slowly, and walked to the door.

'Angus, I know you're there,' she shouted again when he was almost at the door.

When he opened it, she was bending down, about to shout again. She stood up abruptly. 'Oh. Hello.'

'Come in.' He gestured her in.

'I've brought something to eat.' She held up a take-away bag and a bottle of wine with a smile.

'You have an annoying habit of doing the right thing.' He eyed the bag. 'I'm not hungry, but I'll definitely have some wine.'

In the kitchen, she put the take-away bag on the counter and got two plates.

Angus watched her. 'I told you, I'm not hungry.'

'I got your favourite. Thai green curry, sticky rice and peanut satay.'

He stared at her. 'How did you know?' Then he managed a rueful smile. 'Let me guess: you hacked my computer and found my previous orders.'

She smiled, 'nope, I asked Woody.'

He opened the wine, poured two glasses, and pushed one over to her. 'Cheers,' he said, holding up his glass.

'Cheers,' she replied.

She dished out the food, ignoring his earlier comment that he wasn't hungry. They sat on the stools and ate.

'The weather has been warmer than usual for this time of year,' Charlotte commented between mouthfuls.

He nodded.

'The weather report said rain all day, but I haven't seen a drop,' she continued. 'Have you?'

He shook his head.

'I never believe the reports, but I still look in case

they get it right one day. You'd think that with the Met Office being based in Exeter, they'd get our forecast right. I mean, they could look out of the window!'

Angus put a forkful of food into his mouth.

Charlotte sighed. 'If you're just going to be moody and silent, then I'll leave. I thought we'd sorted the money thing out.'

He glanced up at her. 'I'm just feeling despondent about it all. Despite the money, all the leads have run out. I'm not sure we'll find him.'

She reached out and touched his hand. 'We will.'

That made him smile.

Charlotte turned and looked at the conspiracy board. 'We've missed something; we must have. It's probably so obvious that it's literally staring us in the face.' She pointed to a photo of Kenneth. 'The scout leader's not involved. The college tutor was sending kids to a charity shop, and they were peddling drugs, but he didn't know. He's not involved either. Janet is guilty of nothing more than having an affair. But Billy was definitely involved. We should check him out.'

'His murder could be unrelated to the gang,' said Angus. 'There could be a different motive.'

'The only person I haven't been able to get any computer data from was the tutor, David. He'd been meeting students in the cafe and I couldn't hack into his computer.'

'Just because you couldn't hack into his computer doesn't mean he's guilty of anything.' Angus ate some more food.

'It's highly suspicious. These days only people with something to hide use that sort of security.'

'Is that true? He's a computer science tutor,' Angus said

reasonably. 'He's bound to use more security than everyone else.'

Charlotte rolled her eyes. 'Most computer science teachers don't actually know that much about computers.'

'What?' Angus stared at her and lowered his fork to his plate. 'How can they not know much about computers?'

'Because they teach the basics: how computers work, input and output devices and basic programming. They teach little about real-life skills.'

'Are you serious?'

'Absolutely.' She gave a curt nod of her head. 'I need to check his computer. It's the only way to eliminate him. What's David's address?'

'Why?'

'I want to send him some flowers,' she said sarcastically.

Angus sighed. 'I don't know his address. I got his number, though.'

'Can you get one of your mates to look up his address from the phone number?'

'Probably.'

'If not, I'll get brother dear to look into it.'

A few hours later, Angus put the phone down. 'It's a burner phone: unregistered.'

'Even more suspicious. We must follow him and find out where he lives.

'We?' Angus raised an eyebrow.

'He knows who you are!'

'You don't know how to tail someone. I'm good at melting into the background. He won't see me.'

Charlotte studied his face. 'You don't look as if you'd melt into the background.'

'Trust me. I'll tail him and find out his address. You

stay at home until then, and then you can … investigate any flaws in his home Wi-Fi.'

Charlotte sighed. 'All right.'

~

'DAMN IT,' Charlotte said, and closed her laptop. She was sitting in her car at a discreet distance from David's house and been attempting to hack into his Wi-Fi, but it seemed he didn't have one. She'd triangulated all the Wi-Fis listed and none matched his address.

She sat, musing about what to do next. She thought about breaking into his house and stealing his laptop. No, that would be stupid. She'd already crossed the line by hacking into people's Wi-Fi, but burglary? That would be crazy: something she'd never do.

She was about to start the car when a loud knock on the passenger-side window made her jump.

She unlocked the door and Angus got in.

'Jesus, you gave me the fright of my life.' She checked her Apple Watch. 'My heart rate just jumped to 105 bps. It was 75 ten minutes ago.'

'Find anything?' he asked.

'No. He hasn't got Wi-Fi, so there's nothing to hack. Very suspicious, if you ask me.'

'Why?'

'Nobody has wired networks at home these days– well, no one except security-savvy people like me and GCHQ. If he just uses his mobile phone data, there's no way to hack his internet usage. I need to see what he's doing on the computer when he's at the cafe. Shoulder surfing, they call it. He tutors in the cafe a lot, doesn't he?'

'Yes.'

'Good. I'll see what I can learn when he's tutoring there.'

'All right, but at the first sign of trouble, leave.'

The next day, Charlotte was sitting in the cafe opposite the Met Office, sipping her second cup of tea. She'd been there nearly two hours, and she needed the loo. The woman behind the counter had said that David was usually there every afternoon from two o'clock. By four, she was about to give up when he walked in. He ordered a coffee and sat down near her. She couldn't see what he was doing on his laptop, so she went to the counter, got another coffee and sat at a different table with a clear view over his shoulder.

He opened his laptop and typed in a password, then connected to his mobile phone data and typed in a web address.

He went to the website of a local garage: HT Hobart Car Servicing. He navigated a few pages; one showed a car for sale. Then his student arrived, and the lesson began. For an hour they talked about converting binary to hexadecimal and practised using past exam papers. Meanwhile, Charlotte entered the web address into her mobile phone and checked a few pages. None of it seemed out of the ordinary or suspicious. Maybe Angus was right and he wasn't involved. The student left an hour later and shortly afterwards David left too.

She needed to get back to her computer at home and run her analysis program on the Car Servicing website David had been looking at before the student arrived. She'd looked at the code behind the website in the Cafe and found nothing. It was a long shot, and there might be nothing in it, but it was the only thing to go on.

Chapter 27

The next evening, Angus was ready early for Grace's party. He couldn't believe that his daughter was twenty-one already. Where had the time gone? It seemed as if only yesterday she had been a tiny little thing. Lots of people had told him to cherish when she was little because children grew up too quickly. He had taken no notice.

He looked at himself in the mirror. He had wanted to wear a black suit and bow tie, but thought it might be too much. Instead, he opted for his smartest suit, a dark blue pinstripe, with a dark tie and a light-blue shirt.

When he arrived at the community centre, the room was already decked out with balloons and streamers, and the DJ was setting up his gear.

He saw Rhona across the room, talking to the caterers and pointing to various platters of food, then places on the buffet table. He walked over. 'Hello, Rhona.' He kissed her on the cheek. 'No Brian tonight?'

'It's Malcolm, as you know, and Grace didn't want him here.'

Angus wanted to say that Grace was a wise girl, but he bit his tongue.

'She still thinks we're going to get back together.' Rhona raised her eyebrows.

'Need help with anything?' he asked.

'I don't think so. Look, here she is!'

Grace rushed over, and they hugged. She wore a long, dark blue satin dress and her hair was elegantly styled in a long side braid. 'Hi, Dad.'

He took her hands. 'Look at you, all grown up.' He smiled. 'Happy birthday.'

'Thanks, Dad. And thanks for your present–it was brilliant.' She touched the silver necklace he'd given her - its pendant was two silver rings intertwined, one for each decade and a small one that held them in place for the one extra year. 'The Spa vouchers were brilliant too. I'm so glad you're here.'

He squeezed her hands. 'I wouldn't have missed it for the world.'

A couple of hours later, Angus stood at the side of the dance floor, watching. Everyone was slowly getting drunk. He'd spent the time catching up with family, including Rhona's parents, her brother and sister, and their kids. They'd told him how sorry they were that he and Rhona had broken up. Funny how none of them contacted him. They'd also been asking what he was up to now that he'd left the police, and had been interested when he told them he was trying to find that missing boy they kept seeing on social media.

He wanted another beer, but if he had another, he'd be on his way to getting tipsy. He didn't want to make a spectacle of himself and he didn't like the feeling of losing control, so got a cola instead.

Glancing around the room, he saw a woman come into

the hall, and he blinked. That woman was the image of Charlotte. He must be seeing things. He needed to get her out of his head. He was fighting his attraction to her and it was obviously affecting him more than he realised.

The woman moved towards him, weaving around the flailing dancers, and he pushed his glasses up his nose to see her better. She wasn't dressed for a party - she was in jeans and a black jacket.

It was definitely Charlotte.

'What are you doing here?' he shouted into her ear.

'It's nice to see you too,' she shouted back. 'I need to talk to you.' She gestured for him to go outside.

The hallway was much quieter, the noise of the disco muffled by the doors. The smell of cigarette smoke drifted in from outside.

'I've been calling you all evening, but it kept going to voicemail.' She looked him straight in the eye. 'Are you trying to avoid me?'

'I'm at my daughter's twenty-first birthday party, in case you hadn't noticed.' He had brought his phone with him, but put it on silent hours ago. He had wanted to give Grace his full attention, not interrupt the night with work. Not that he'd expected any break-throughs.

Charlotte looked him up and down. 'You look very dashing tonight.' She didn't wait for him to answer. 'I've had a breakthrough with the tutor, David. He's definitely involved.'

'David is? How do you know? And how did you know where I was? Did you track my phone?'

'I'll explain if you come back to my house.' She turned towards the door, but Angus didn't move.

'I'm not leaving. It's my daughter's party.'

She stared at him. 'You have to come. David is meeting a gang member tonight.'

'What do you mean?'

'I'll explain on the way. I'll drive.'

'I'm going nowhere.'

'I thought you wanted to find Daniel?'

'I do.'

'This is the best lead we've had. David is definitely involved. Why do I need to tell you twice?'

Angus's head spun. He loved his daughter beyond words, and this was her twenty-first. It would only happen once. On the other hand, Grace was half-drunk and in the throes of the party. She probably wouldn't notice he'd gone until the end. He could go and tell her he was leaving … or he could slip away and be back before she even noticed.

He glanced at the door. 'What time are they meeting?'

'Ten pm.'

He checked his watch: nine thirty. The party finished at midnight. He had plenty of time. 'All right, but I'll need you to bring me back.'

'No problem.'

He turned and opened the door—

'Running off with your girlfriend? Maybe I should have given her an invite too, and then you'd hang around for longer than five minutes.' Rhona stood in the doorway of the main room, glaring at him.

'She's not my girlfriend; I told you.'

Rhona folded her arms. 'I don't believe you.'

'She's working on the case with me. We've had a break-through.'

Rhona shook her head. 'You never change, do you? I thought maybe things would have been different once you'd left the police. But here you are, putting your job before your family. Again.'

'I won't be long.'

'Well, I won't cover for you. If she asks, I'll tell her the truth.'

'I'd expect nothing less from you.' He turned away from her, and they left.

As soon as they were on their way, Charlotte began explaining. 'As you know, I went to the cafe to monitor David's internet traffic. He was still using a VPN, so I couldn't hack his computer, but I looked at his screen and he went on a website of a local mechanic. He was looking at cars to buy—one car in particular.'

She was driving west towards the city centre. 'But he doesn't drive, does he? You said that day when you first spoke to him he left saying he was catching a bus and I saw him at the bus stop just down from the cafe. So why was he checking out cars?'

'Maybe he wanted a car because he's fed up with the awful public transport in Devon.'

She ignored that. 'When I got home, I analysed the web pages he was looking at and found nothing unusual. But then I looked at the image files. They have steno-graphic messages hidden in them!' She beamed at him.

'Stego-what messages?'

'Stenographic hidden messages. It's a secret message hidden in an image or an audio file. A classic way to hide things in plain sight, especially over the internet. You take an image and run it through an algorithm that embeds the message in the file. It alters the image, but not enough for humans to see. It's virtually impossible to uncover unless you know what you're looking for. And watching David looking at that website showed me exactly where to find it. I ran the images of the cars through some standard stenography cracking tools and bingo! They'd used one of the basic ones. Schoolboy error. Amateurish, actually.'

Angus wasn't sure if he'd had too much to drink or if

he was just stupid, but he had no idea what she was talking about.

'OK, so hidden messages in photos on a website. What did the message say?'

'10pm. Hobarts.'

'And that's where we're heading?'

'Yep.'

'You think David is meeting the gang members?'

'I'm certain. Why else would he be looking at the exact image with the message?'

Chapter 28

Charlotte pulled up near the garage and switched the car engine off.

It was a quarter to ten. There was a dim light in the garage's window. 'What do we do now?' she asked Angus.

'We watch, and wait.'

At five minutes to ten, they saw a dark figure approach the garage and go in. They both recognised David the tutor.

'That's him!' Charlotte said under her breath.

Angus turned to her. 'Well done.'

'What happens now?'

'Nothing. We wait for him to come out and see who else comes and goes.'

Ten minutes later, David came out of the garage with another man, his face concealed by a hoody. The man locked the door behind him and walked in the opposite direction to David.

'You follow David in the car,' said Angus. 'Don't, under any circumstances, get out of the car or talk to him. I'm going to follow the other man. Text me where he goes.'

Charlotte turned to him. 'How can I follow him in the car?'

'Turn the lights off and follow at a distance. Use the electric engine so he doesn't hear you. He's probably going home, anyway. He's heading in that direction.' And with that, he got out of the car and was gone.

'Shit,' Charlotte said. David was walking down the road. She switched the engine on; it was as quiet as a mouse. She drove slowly, following him.

ANGUS HAD BEEN good at following suspects during his years in the police. He felt alive again. Covert work was the thing he'd liked most.

He followed the man at a comfortable distance past houses and shops, past the Catholic church, and then saw him go into a house on West Street.

Angus considered what to do next. As he did, a light went on in the front room. Whoever he was, he was alone.

He felt a buzz; and wasn't sure if it was the drink in his system or his elation at following the suspect. He knocked on the door and it opened almost immediately. A man stood there.

Kenneth the Scout leader.

They stared at each other. Kenneth tried to shut the door, but Angus put his foot in the way and shouldered the door open.

'Hello, Kenneth.' Angus stepped inside and Kenneth backed away.

'Er, what are you doing here?' He glanced around shiftily.

'I'm still looking for Daniel. And I think you know where he is.'

'I–I don't,' Kenneth said in a worried voice.

'You do, and you're going to tell me.'

Kenneth backed into a chair and sat down in it. 'I really don't know where he is.'

'You and David are involved in his disappearance.'

He stared at Angus. 'How did you know about David?'

'You've been reading his hidden messages in image files on the HT Hobart Garage website.'

'But those are a secret!'

'Tell me where he is.'

'I told you, I don't know,' he gabbled.

'Tell me who does.'

'I can't. They're blackmailing me.'

'With what?'

He paused for a moment, his face full of shock. 'With the same thing as Daniel.' He swallowed. 'They got me to…' His gaze was everywhere but on Angus. 'I did things on the webcam and they blackmailed me into helping them. I didn't want to do it, but I had no choice.'

'There's always a choice.' Angus shook his head in disbelief. 'What are you doing here?' His voice sounded accusing, even to himself.

'They're making me deliver drugs for them. That's what they're making Daniel do, too. I pick up the package here. Someone is coming soon. I have to take the drugs to one of their safe houses.'

'Have you seen Daniel?'

'Not recently.'

'So you have seen him?'

'Last week.'

Angus grabbed his collar and half-lifted him from the chair. 'Where is he?'

'I swear I don't know. They sent him to Newcastle last week. They've been getting him to move drugs around the country and got me to give him his instructions at first to make him do it. I don't know if he's coming back. They don't tell me much.'

'Where was he staying before?'

'At one of the gang's safe houses.'

'What's the address?'

Kenneth paused, and Angus could tell he was about to break. Then the spell broke, and he shook his head. 'I can't tell you. They'll kill me, like Billy.'

'You can either tell me now or tell the police when they interrogate you. You should think about Daniel. If I tell the police, you helped me find him, they'll go easy on you. Especially as you're being blackmailed, too.'

Kenneth's eyes were wide, his arms crossed in front of him like a barrier.

Angus softened his voice. 'Come on, tell me.'

'David is high in the organisation. He finds young people like Daniel. That's how he picked him.'

'Through his tuition work.'

Kenneth nodded. 'They'll kill me when they find out I told you that.'

'Not if we catch them,' Angus said. 'Who else is involved in the gang?'

'I don't know. There are others, but they never told me their names. David is the only one I have contact with.'

'How many kids have they got working for them?'

Kenneth shrugged. 'Four or five around Exeter.'

Angus stared at him, trying to assess whether he was telling the truth. 'Are they dropping something off here soon?'

'In about fifteen mins.'

'You're early, then.'

'They don't like me to be late.'

Angus stood over Kenneth; he was losing patience with him. 'Where is Daniel?'

'He's in a house in Pinhoe.'

'Address?'

Kenneth stared at Angus, silent.

'Come on, tell me.'

Kenneth exhaled heavily. '26 Queen Street.'

'Make the pickup as usual; they can't suspect anything is up.'

'What are you doing?'

'I'm going to the safe house to get Daniel.'

If he'd been in the police, he'd have called for backup and had Kenneth taken to the nearest station. But his primary concern now was Charlotte. David was a key gang member and Charlotte was following him...

Angus went outside, then around the corner and dialled Charlotte's number. It rang eight times before going to voicemail.

'Hi, this is Charlotte. I'm either ignoring you or I can't talk right now. Leave a message, and if I feel like it, I'll call you back.'

Angus smiled, despite his anxiety. Typical Charlotte.

'Charlotte, it's Angus. Call me back asap, it's important. I've got a likely location for Daniel and I'm going there now. Stay away from David: he's dangerous.'

He stuffed his phone in his pocket and ran as fast as he could. If he'd had the car, it would have been easy. A taxi was out of the question this time of night.

She hadn't answered. Something's wrong, I know it.

Every road was longer than they ever were when he ran on them to keep fit.

Finally, he reached Queen Street. He slowed down, peering to see the numbers of the houses.

Chapter 29

Charlotte watched David hurry away. He was definitely involved in the gang, but she wasn't sure how much. Whatever happened, she couldn't lose sight of him.

After turning into a residential area, he went down an alley.

'Shit.' The car wouldn't fit down there.

She pulled over and got out, quietly moving towards the dark alley. She stopped at the entrance.

She hated the dark. Hated alleys. She shouldn't even be out of the car, let alone thinking of going in it.

She gritted her teeth and began walking.

Inside the alley were different gates leading to different houses. A bang was heard further up, followed by a security light turning on. She ran up to the gate and peered over, but couldn't see anything. She forced herself to calm down, trying to remember her therapist, Misty's calming voice. Overcoming her fear of this was something she really needed to do.

'Looking for me?' Her heart skipped a beat. She turned

around and came face to face with David. 'Why are you following me?' He came closer, looming over her.

Charlotte stood still for a moment, stunned. 'Er, sorry, I lost my way. Do you know the way to Domino's Pizza?' Damn, that was a stupid thing to say.

'Darling, I know you were following me. First in your car, and now on foot.'

'Follow you?' She swallowed. 'Why would I follow you?'

He lunged and grabbed her arm, then pulled out a knife. 'This way.' He forced her through the back gate and into a house. The door led straight into a kitchen.

He pulled a chair out from a round kitchen table. 'Sit down.'

She did as she was told. He was still holding the knife, and it looked sharp.

He pulled the blind down, took out his phone, and dialled a number. 'Where are you? Hurry up, you idiot… Yeah, all right. Be quick, I've got trouble here.' He ended the call, then walked to the kitchen door. 'Come down!' he shouted up.

Shortly afterwards there was a rumble of noise in the room above, then heavy footsteps down the stairs.

The door opened.

'Daniel!' Charlotte gasped.

'Who are you?' Daniel looked at her.

'I've been looking for you!'

'Shut up,' David snapped.

Charlotte's phone rang in her pocket. She winced: she should have put it on silent.

David spun around. 'Give me the phone.'

She sighed, put her hand in her pocket and put the ringing, buzzing phone on the table.

David picked it up and looked at the screen. 'Angus Darrow. So you're working with the ex-police officer.'

She shrugged. 'He's a friend, that's all.'

'And you're following me.'

'Pure coincidence,' she said, trying to keep her voice level.

'You're a terrible liar.'

'Everyone tells me that. I must practise.'

He took the phone to the sink and dropped it into the washing-up bowl. It made a loud plop and a few moments later, the ringing stopped.

Charlotte didn't react. Angry men were more likely to calm down if you didn't react. She'd learnt that from Helena.

David turned to Daniel. 'You've got another job. This is the address. Be a good boy and do it quickly.' He put the knife on the counter.

Daniel took the paper David held out. 'Shetland. That's on a boat. I hate boats.'

'I don't care,' David said. 'You'll do as you're told.' He slapped Daniel on the back of the head.

'Don't do that!' Charlotte cried. 'Daniel, you have to go home to your parents. Don't worry, I'll look after you. We can protect you.'

'I'm warning you!' David stepped towards her, jaw clenched.

'Or what?' Charlotte stood up. 'You're a nasty bully and I hate bullies. Always have.'

'Sit down.' Daniel flinched as David's voice rose almost to a shout.

'You'll have to make me.' She placed a hand on her hip and lifted her chin.

He stepped forward, hand raised. Charlotte ducked, twisted away and grabbed for the knife....

Her fingers were centimetres away when David knocked the knife out of reach.

'Get it, Daniel,' she screamed. 'Stop him!'

David grabbed her and threw her aside. She fell on the table hard, winding herself, but struggled upright to see Daniel pointing the knife at David.

'I can't do this anymore,' he said. His hand was trembling. 'I want to go home.'

'Don't be stupid, Daniel. Remember, we've got those videos of you.'

'I don't care,' he said, his entire arm shaking. 'I don't care, I want to go home. I want my mum.'

'I want my muuuum,' David echoed, sneering.

'Shut up,' Daniel shouted.

David edged towards Daniel. 'You can go home soon. Just a few more jobs, and then you can go.'

'They'll never let you go, Daniel,' said Charlotte. Daniel stared at her, eyes wide. 'They'll always get you to do their bidding. Then they'll kill you, like they did your Uncle Billy. You can help bring them down.' Charlotte moved closer. 'I'm a cyber expert; I can help you find and delete the videos. And your mum's desperate to have you back. She misses you so much. That's why I'm here: they hired me to find you. They're desperate.'

'Give the knife to me, Daniel, and I'll forget this silly little episode,' said David. 'Just one more job, Daniel, then you can go home.' He held his hand out, palm upwards. 'Give. Me. The knife.'

Daniel stood still, hand still shaking, pointing it at David.

Charlotte's brain whirred. She was out of David's line of sight now. She had to do something, and quickly. If Daniel gave David the knife, it was all over, and she would end up like Billy. Dead. David was over six feet tall; he'd overpower her easily if she tried to grab him or fight. She looked around for something she could use to incapacitate him. Her eyes fell on the cooker, and she discreetly reached out a hand.

The object secured, she swung it at David as hard as she could. But instead of going for his head, she did what her brother had taught her long ago: she hit him in the place that would hurt the most.

The shins.

There was a loud crack as the metal saucepan hit bone, and David crumpled to the floor with a loud scream. 'You bitch!' He writhed on the floor, clutching his legs.

Charlotte and Daniel both stood watching him for a moment before Charlotte remembered there was more to do. She took the knife from Daniel, pulled out her spare mobile phone from the inside pocket of her jacket, and dialled 999.

She explained the situation to the police call centre, her voice rising above David's cries of agony. At one point, he tried to stand up, but his knees gave way and he fell on the floor again.

Charlotte ended the call and looked down at him. 'Is there any rope, Daniel, or anything we can use to tie him up? We don't know how long the police will take to get here.'

Daniel, who had sat down at the kitchen table, pointed to a drawer. She opened it and among the general junk found a piece of thin rope.

A few minutes later, they heard a thump on the door.

'That was quick! Let the police in, Daniel.' Charlotte had tied David's legs together and was now tying up his wrists as he screamed obscenities at her.

'You've broken my shin, you utter bitch…'

Charlotte smiled, adrenaline searing through her.

The front door opened and a moment later, Angus appeared in the kitchen doorway.

'Angus!' She threw herself at him and hugged him. 'Thank God.'

He held her for a few moments, then drew back. 'Are you all right?' he asked, his blue eyes scanning her face.

She nodded. 'A bit shocked, but I'll be all right. I thought you were the police.'

'What happened?'

'David here will need medical help. I overpowered him.'

'So I see,' said Angus, his eyes narrowing.

'The police should be here any moment.' Charlotte stood back, admiring her work as David glared at her and swore.

Then Angus saw Daniel stood in the back corner of the room. 'You found him! Daniel, we've been searching for you.'

'I want to go home,' said Daniel. 'Can I go home?'

Angus smiled at him. 'You can. I promise.'

Chapter 30

A couple of days later, Charlotte sat next to Angus in his living room. Daniel and his parents sat opposite.

Mary Cray wore black leggings, a loose pale-blue top, and she had a broad smile on her face as she reached for her mug of tea. She had even put on make-up, and she glowed. Douglas Cray also looked smarter than before in black jeans and a checked shirt. He said little, but his demeanour and smile showed how relieved he was.

On the coffee table between them sat a tray of tea things and a plate of biscuits. Daniel picked up a custard cream and put it in his mouth in one go.

'We're so grateful to have our Daniel back. Aren't we, Danny?' Mary said, sitting back and stroking his arm. Daniel said nothing but stared straight ahead, chewing. 'He's still trying to process it all,' she continued. 'He'll be himself soon. The key thing is he's back with us. He's promised never to go away again. Haven't you, love?'

Mary linked her arm with Daniel's. He didn't respond.

Charlotte smiled. 'Have the police charged David?'

Charlotte had asked Mary, but it was Angus who

responded. 'I spoke to the Police earlier and yes, they've charged him along with the drugs, kidnapping, false imprisonment. They're probably going to charge him with Billy's murder, too.'

'They think he did it, then?' Charlotte poured milk into her mug and took a sip.

He nodded. 'They found forensic evidence which led back to him. Apparently David was an alias and he's wanted for several other crimes under his real name. ABH and drugs, that sort of thing.'

'Did they get proof or did he confess?'

'He hasn't confessed, but forensics found traces of Billy's blood in David's house. They think the murder took place there. They've apprehended fifteen people from the gang who were pushing drugs all over the country, and they found the other two missing boys in London.'

'How awful.' Charlotte commented. 'So David killed Billy because he was trying to get Daniel out of the gang?'

'Apparently so. Billy only got involved in the first place because he needed the money for gambling debts. When they targeted Danny, he threatened to go to the police. That's when he killed him.'

'He brought it on himself.' They all looked round at Douglas in surprise. 'He always had a problem with gambling.'

Angus and Charlotte exchanged glances. Charlotte wanted to say that no one deserved to be murdered, whatever they'd done, but kept quiet. 'What about Kenneth the Scout leader?' she asked instead.

'It's doubtful he'll be charged with anything serious,' said Angus. 'He was forced into it too.'

'When Janet found out, she was the angriest I've ever seen her,' said Mary. 'I didn't know about their affair. I can't believe she didn't tell me. She always told me everything or at least I thought she did. She admitted it all to me and vowed to break it off. He lied about Daniel. He could have gone to the police, but he didn't.' Her voice became high pitched and when she'd stopped speaking, her lips were pursed.

They all sat silent for a moment. 'Can we go now?' asked Daniel.

'In a minute, Danny. I still haven't thanked Mr Darrow for all his work.' She turned to Angus. 'I'll never be able to thank you enough, Mr Darrow. Tom came round last night to check on Danny. He's such a great godfather to him, and I'm so glad he persuaded you to help us.'

Angus indicated to Charlotte. 'Charlotte and her computer skills cracked it.'

They all looked at her. 'We're so grateful,' Mary continued. 'We've still got thousands left over from the crowd funder. I wish I could find out who donated the money so that I could thank them.'

'What will you do with the leftover money?' Angus asked, glancing at Charlotte.

Mary frowned. 'We're not sure what to do with it. I'd give it back if I could.'

Douglas stared at her with a concerned expression.

'Well, I'm sure the donor would be happy for you to keep it,' said Charlotte. 'Maybe you could put it towards giving Daniel a good start in life. Or perhaps a holiday for you all?'

'Do you think so?' Mary bit her bottom lip.

'Absolutely.'

'I hadn't thought of a holiday. You've always wanted to go to Disney World, haven't you, Danny?'

'There you are: you can have the holiday of a lifetime,' said Charlotte.

'I want to go to the Star Wars bit,' said Daniel. 'They have people dressed up as storm troopers.'

Charlotte nodded. 'I took my boys there about six years ago and they loved it. Perfect for Star Wars fans.'

Mary finished her tea and put her cup down. 'Well, we should leave you in peace now...'

Angus saw them out, then returned to the living room. 'Look, what I said was true. I wouldn't have been able to find him without you.'

'I'm a super-genius. Tell everyone you know.' She grinned at him.

He laughed. 'I will.'

'I like to be indispensable.' She met his eyes. 'It felt great to have a purpose, and I can't tell you how much it's helped me. The last year or so has been a haze of anger and self-loathing, and now I can see the light at the end of the tunnel.'

'What are you planning to do now?' He stood close, facing her.

She shrugged. 'Hang around and help you.'

'I can't afford to pay you.'

'I don't need the money, I've told you.'

'It doesn't seem right.' He shook his head, but he was smiling. It gave her hope.

'As long as it's helping my mental health, I'll stick around for free. I can't work in my sector for another three years and eight months, not that I'm counting, so you've got me until then.' She smiled. 'I could teach you everything I know, if you like.'

Angus put his hands up in surrender. 'Thanks, but I'll stick to blissful ignorance.'

'It's never too late to switch careers, you know.'

'I'd rather stack shelves at Tesco. On the night shift.'

She rolled her eyes. 'After a couple of weeks, you'd die of boredom. So you're stuck with me for the foreseeable.'

Angus looked at his watch. 'I'm not chucking you out, but I need to go. I've got workmen coming to the flats.'

'Can I come with you? I'd love to see them.'

He nodded.

Grigore drove them in the Bentley. He didn't give Angus suspicious glances in the rear-view mirror anymore, which was a bonus.

When they entered the flats, a couple of workmen were finishing off. The partition walls had been put in, the carpet laid, and the walls and ceilings decorated.

Angus stood there, mouth open, as one of the workmen walked over to Charlotte. 'Hello Mrs Beavin. That's great timing. We've just finished.'

She beamed at him. 'Pete, you're an absolute star. I can't thank you enough. Though don't call me Mrs Beavin anymore. I'm not using my bastard husband's name. It literally makes me want to vomit. It's Miss Lockwood.'

'No problem, Miss Lockwood. The extra cash certainly helped.' He winked at her.

Charlotte turned to Angus, whose mouth was still open. 'Surprise! Now that the flats are finished, you can concentrate on doing investigations with me.'

Angus waited until Pete had left the room. 'Charlotte, this absolutely takes the biscuit. What do you think you're doing?'

'I made sure the flats were finished. You said you were having problems with getting hold of proper workmen, so I got Pete and his mates to finish them off for you.'

Angus took a deep breath, and his face reddened. 'These are my flats. I can't believe the barefaced cheek.'

'Cheek? I told you the other day: I need this. It's part of my recovery, and I need you focused.'

'Is there any aspect of my life that you haven't interfered with? Would you like to arrange a date for me with one of your friends?'

Charlotte winced. 'I can guarantee I will never arrange a date for you with one of my friends.' She emphasised the word 'never'. 'Anyway, I'm not paying for it: you are. I knew you'd get all precious about me paying, so they'll be billing you, not me. I just gave them a small incentive to come now and work quickly. That's all, I promise. I won't interfere anymore. Guide's Honour.' She held two fingers up to her forehead in the Girl Guide salute.

He gave her a look of incredulity, remembering that she'd only been a Guide for two weeks. 'If you want to continue working with me, we need some ground rules. No more interfering in my life. I have my pride, you know.'

'So you want to continue working with me?' She smiled.

He shifted from foot to foot, then sighed. 'Alright. You were really helpful with all your tech knowledge.'

Charlotte squealed, jumped up and down clapping her hands, then kissed him on the cheek. 'Thank you!'

He walked around the room, checking their work. 'They've done a fantastic job.'

'Of course they have,' she grinned. 'Hey, let's go to that new Thai restaurant near the Cathedral to celebrate. I've been dying to try it. Will you come with me? I hate eating alone.'

Angus nodded. 'You can help me search out an estate agent to advertise the flats.'

'Absolutely, I have a friend who's an estate agent, she'll be able to find you some nice tenants. I'll call her later.'

The End.

～

DEAR READER, I hope you enjoyed the first in the series. It would be brilliant if you could leave a review where you bought it because it helps readers find my books.

If you want more from Charlotte and Angus, the second book is available :

Exe Factor:

When Private Investigator Charlotte Lockwood's friend Katrina is Cat-fished, she is asked to hunt down who was behind the scam. But when the Cat-fisher is found murdered Katrina is the prime suspect. Together with her partner Angus Darrow, they must get to the truth to exonerate Katrina.

Sign up to my newsletter on my website to get a FREE Lockwood and Darrow short story.

www.suzybussell.com

Suzy xx

Acknowledgments

Many thanks to my amazing and supportive husband and to Liz Hedgecock, my editor and mentor, who also writes mysteries - check her books out!

About the Author

Suzy started writing at the age of thirty when she penned her first story – a fan fiction – and then graduated onto writing her own characters and tales.

In 2019, she found herself unable to silence the persistent voices of Charlotte and Angus in her thoughts, their vivid characters forcing her hand to starting the 'Lockwood and Darrow' series.

Originally from Hertfordshire, she's called Devon home for two decades. Its picturesque landscapes and unique character have embedded themselves in almost every story she's penned.

She has a background in computing and a keen interest in technology which naturally weaves it's way into her plots to add a touch of modern intrigue. The world of technology has always fascinated her, and merging this with her passion for storytelling felt like a natural progression.

Currently, she lives close to the sea with an amazing and supportive husband, three sons, and two Snowshoe cats. When she's not writing, she loves swimming and playing her Violin.

Made in United States
North Haven, CT
22 January 2024